FOX & RABBIT

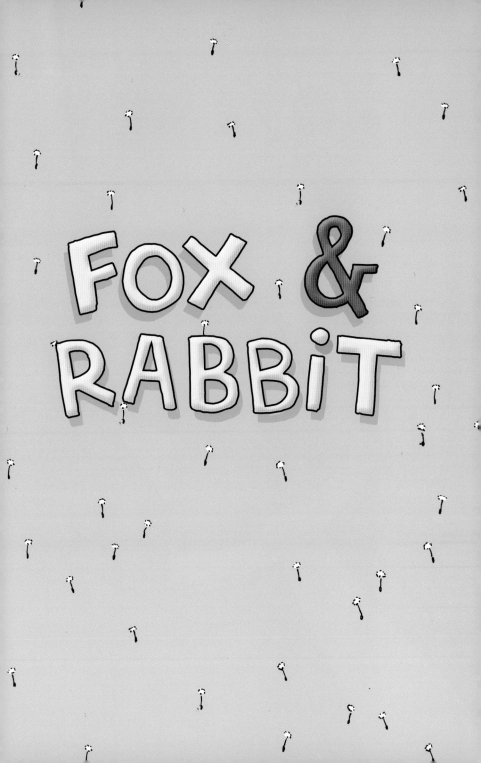

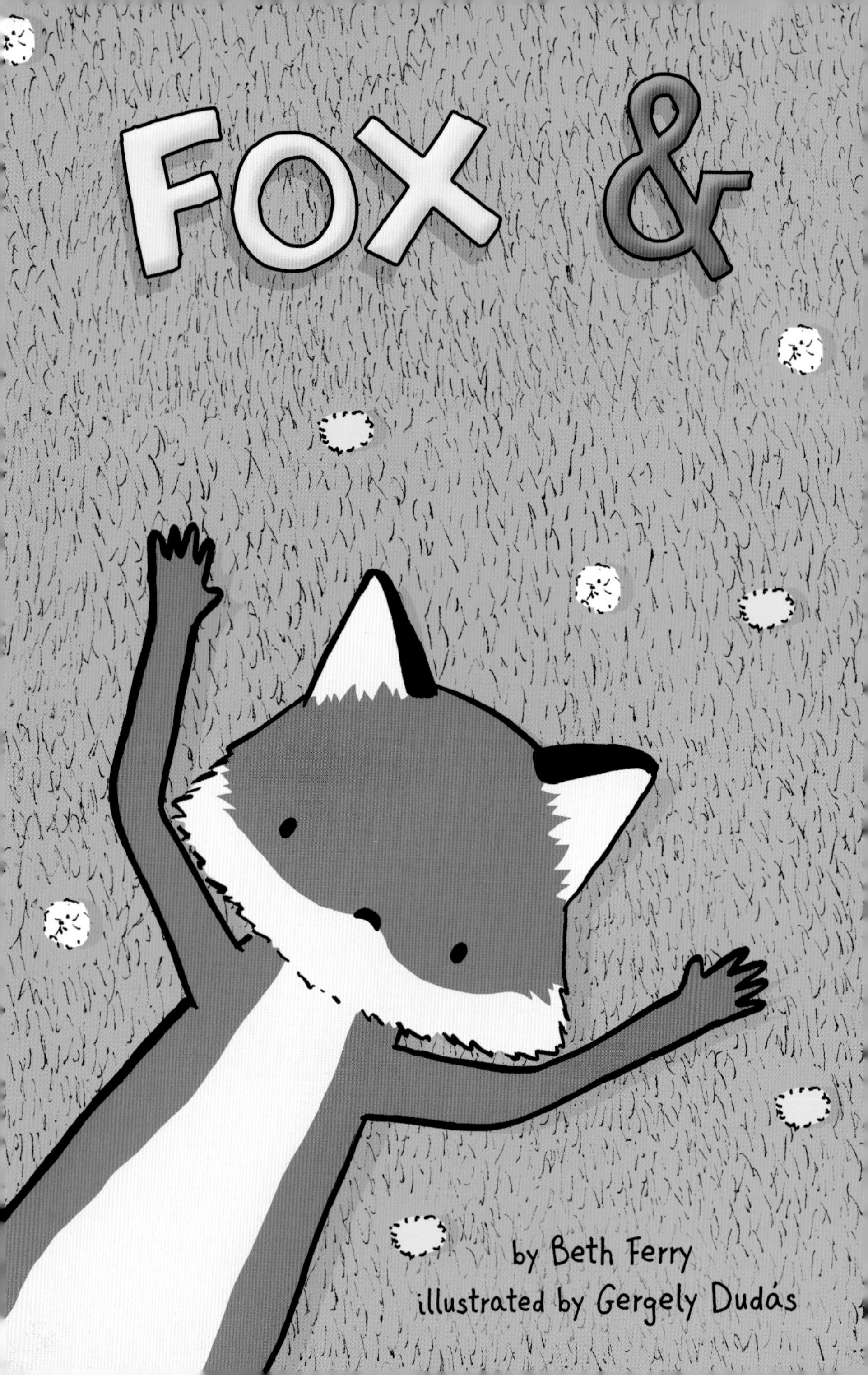
FOX &
by Beth Ferry
illustrated by Gergely Dudás

RABBIT

AMULET BOOKS · NEW YORK

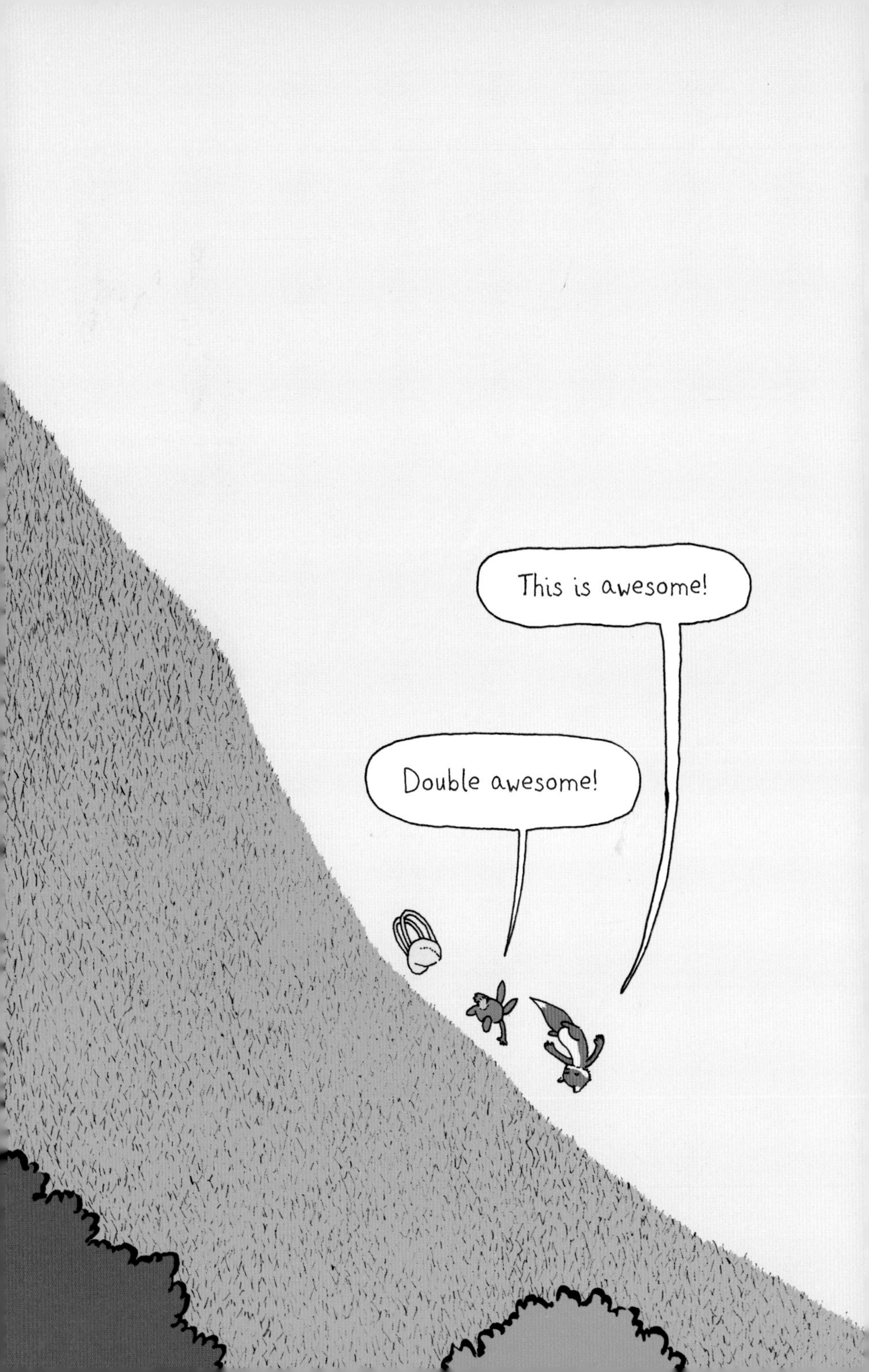
This is awesome!
Double awesome!

CONTENTS

STORY ONE

FAIR, FIREWORKS & FRED

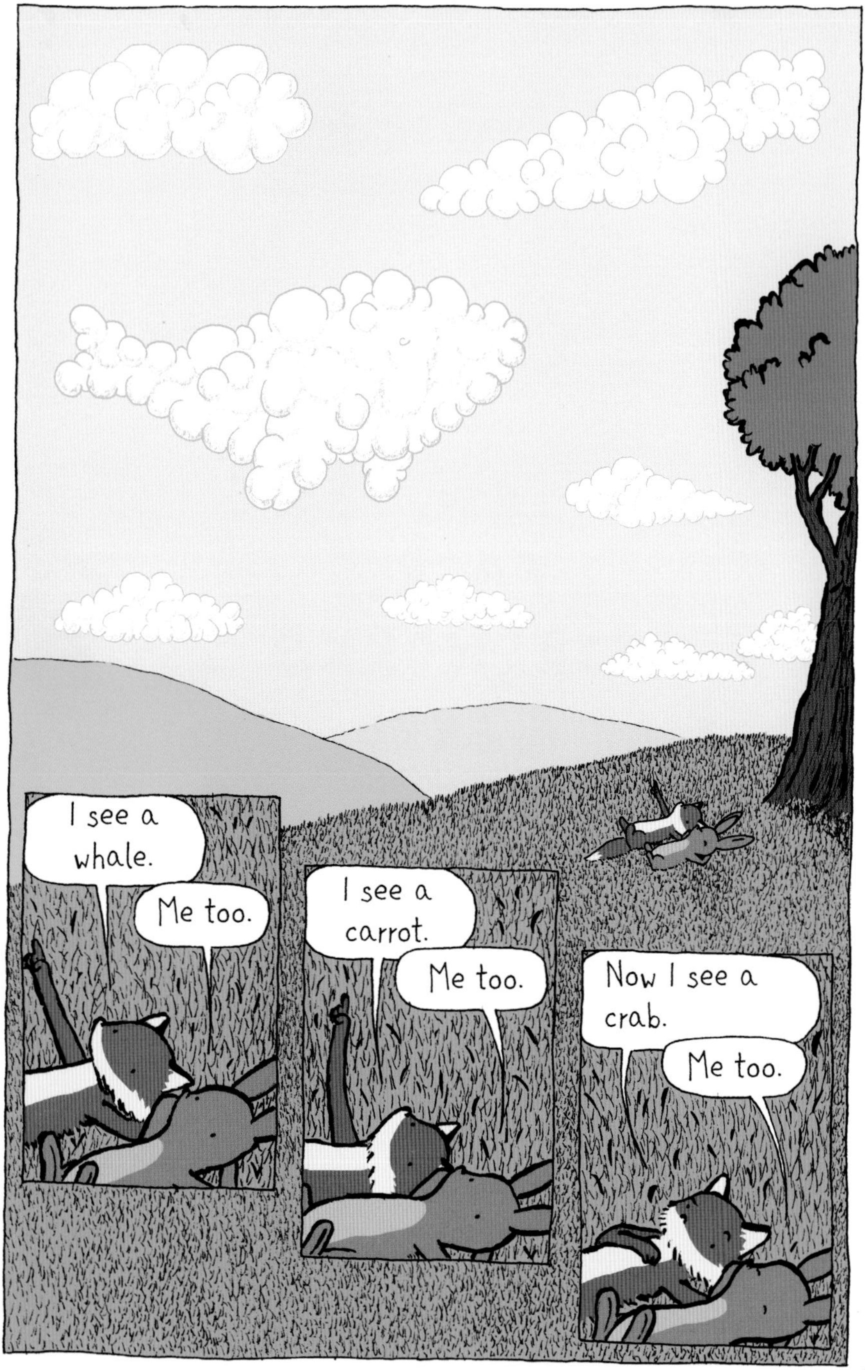
I see a whale.
Me too.
I see a carrot.
Me too.
Now I see a crab.
Me too.

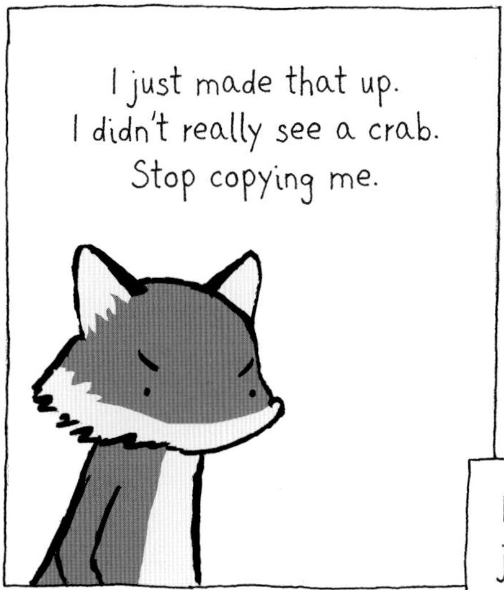
I just made that up.
I didn't really see a crab.
Stop copying me.

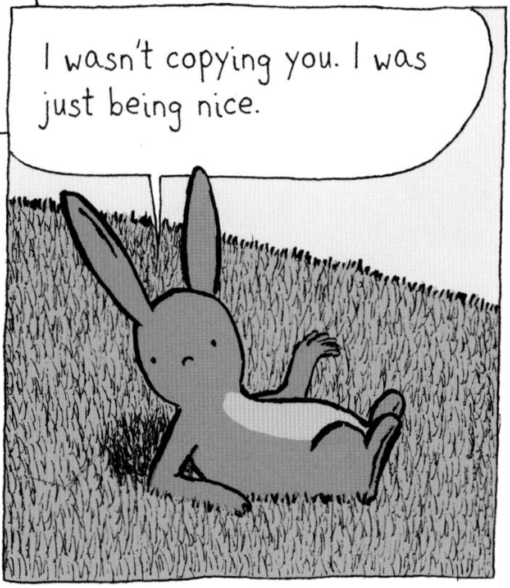
I wasn't copying you. I was just being nice.

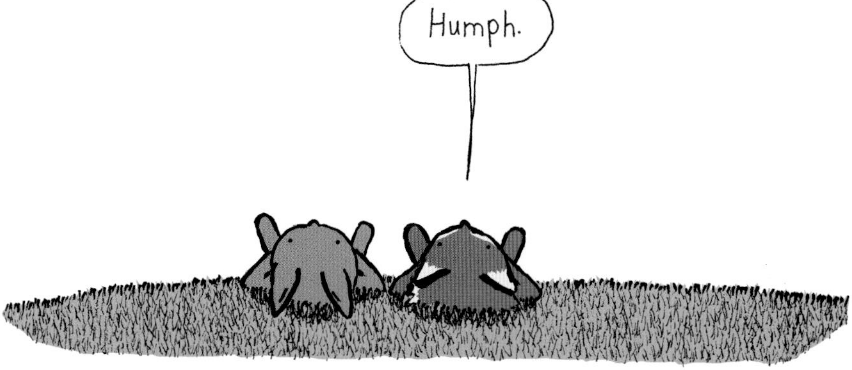
Humph.

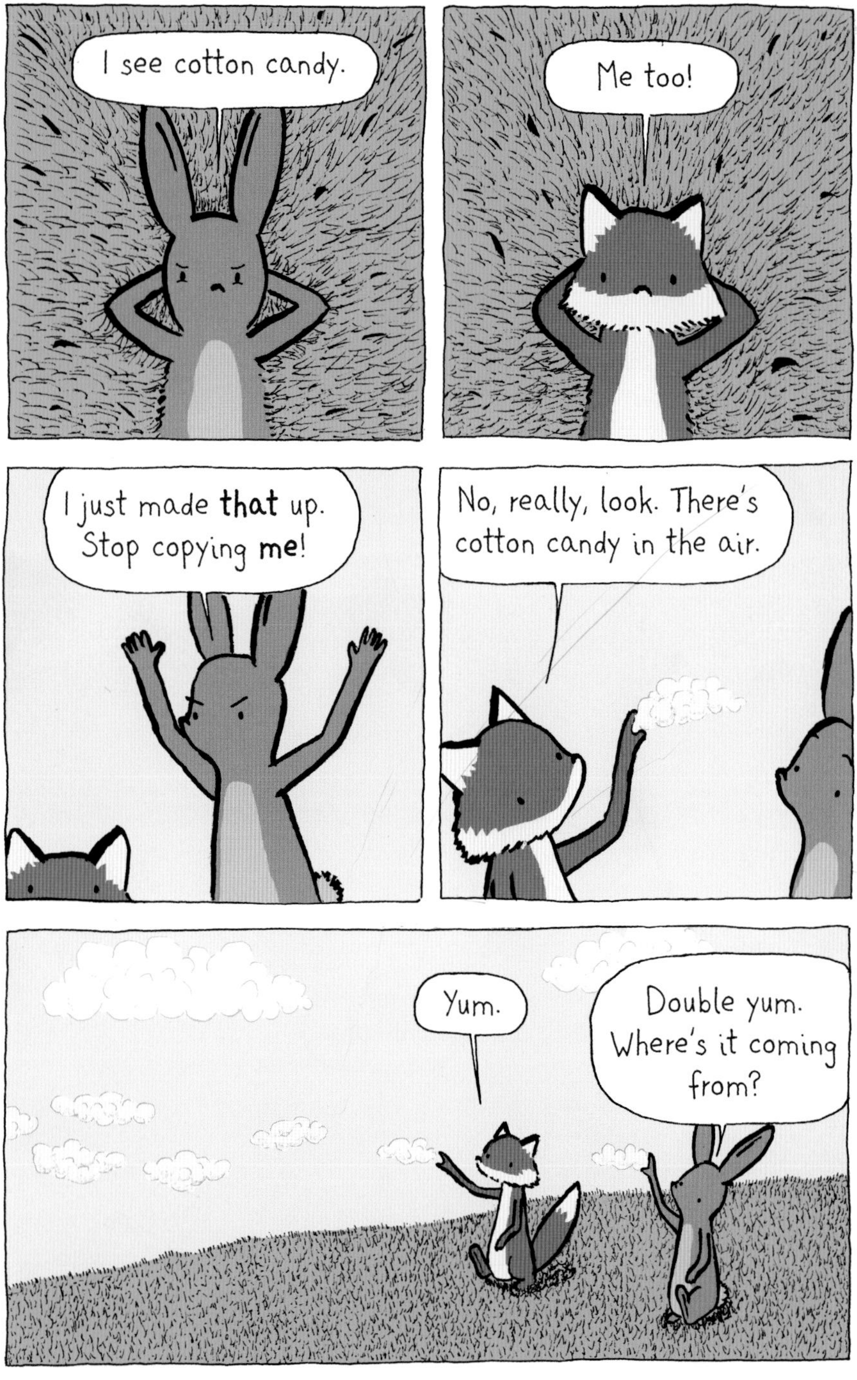
I see cotton candy.
Me too!
I just made **that** up. Stop copying **me**!
No, really, look. There's cotton candy in the air.
Yum.
Double yum. Where's it coming from?

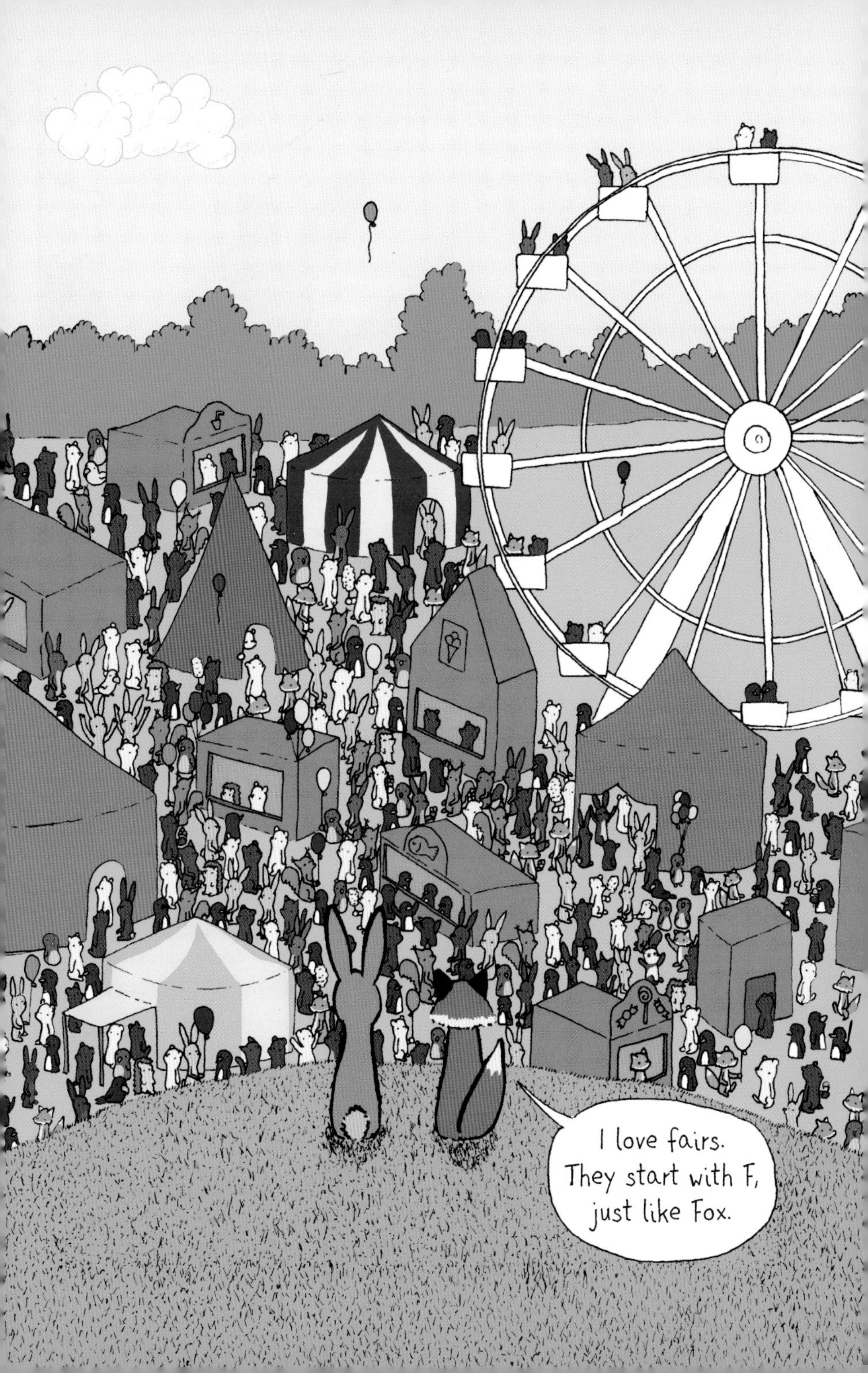
I love fairs. They start with F, just like Fox.

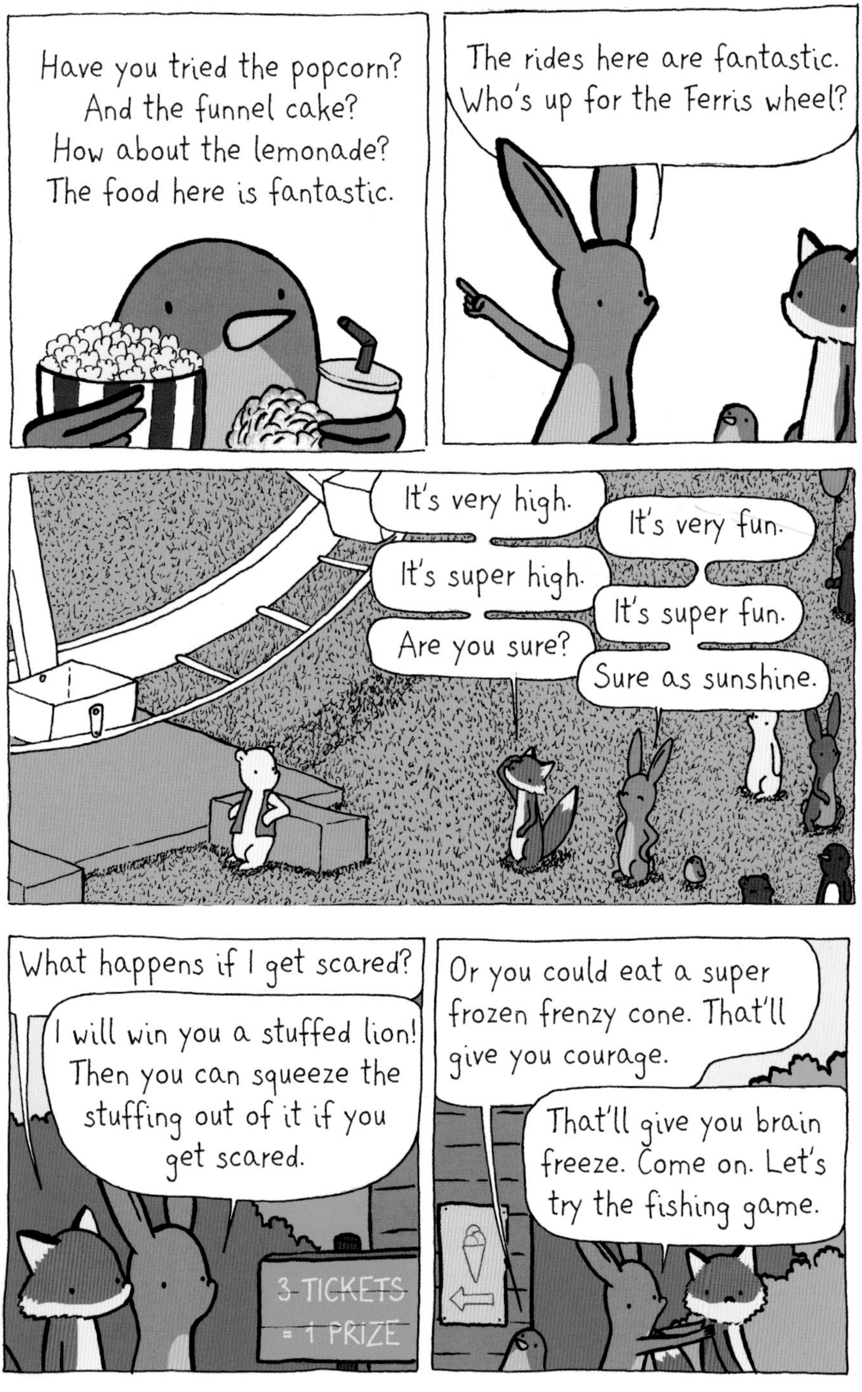
Have you tried the popcorn? And the funnel cake? How about the lemonade? The food here is fantastic.
The rides here are fantastic. Who's up for the Ferris wheel?
It's very high.
It's very fun.
It's super high.
It's super fun.
Are you sure?
Sure as sunshine.
What happens if I get scared?
I will win you a stuffed lion! Then you can squeeze the stuffing out of it if you get scared.
3 TICKETS = 1 PRIZE
Or you could eat a super frozen frenzy cone. That'll give you courage.
That'll give you brain freeze. Come on. Let's try the fishing game.

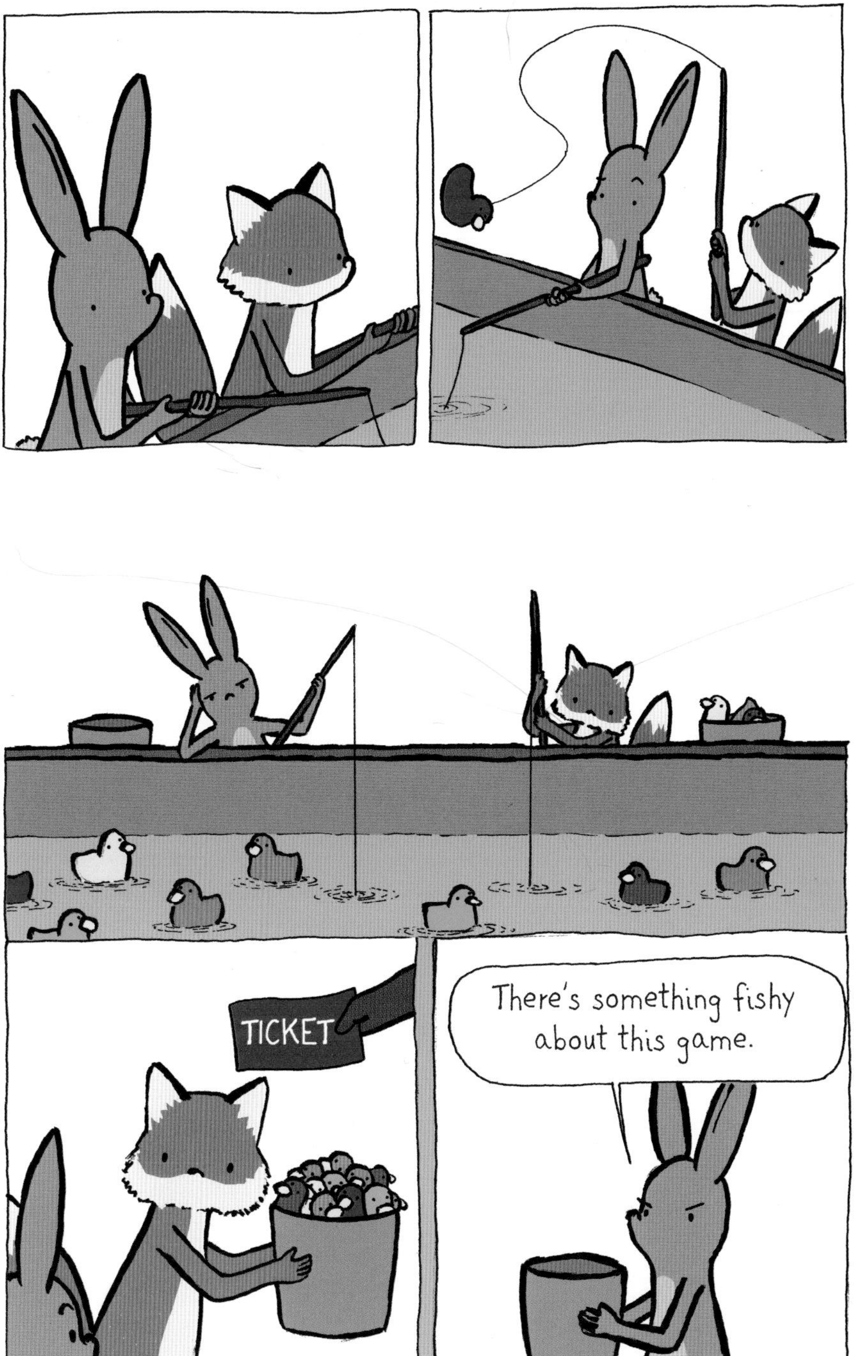
TICKET
There's something fishy about this game.

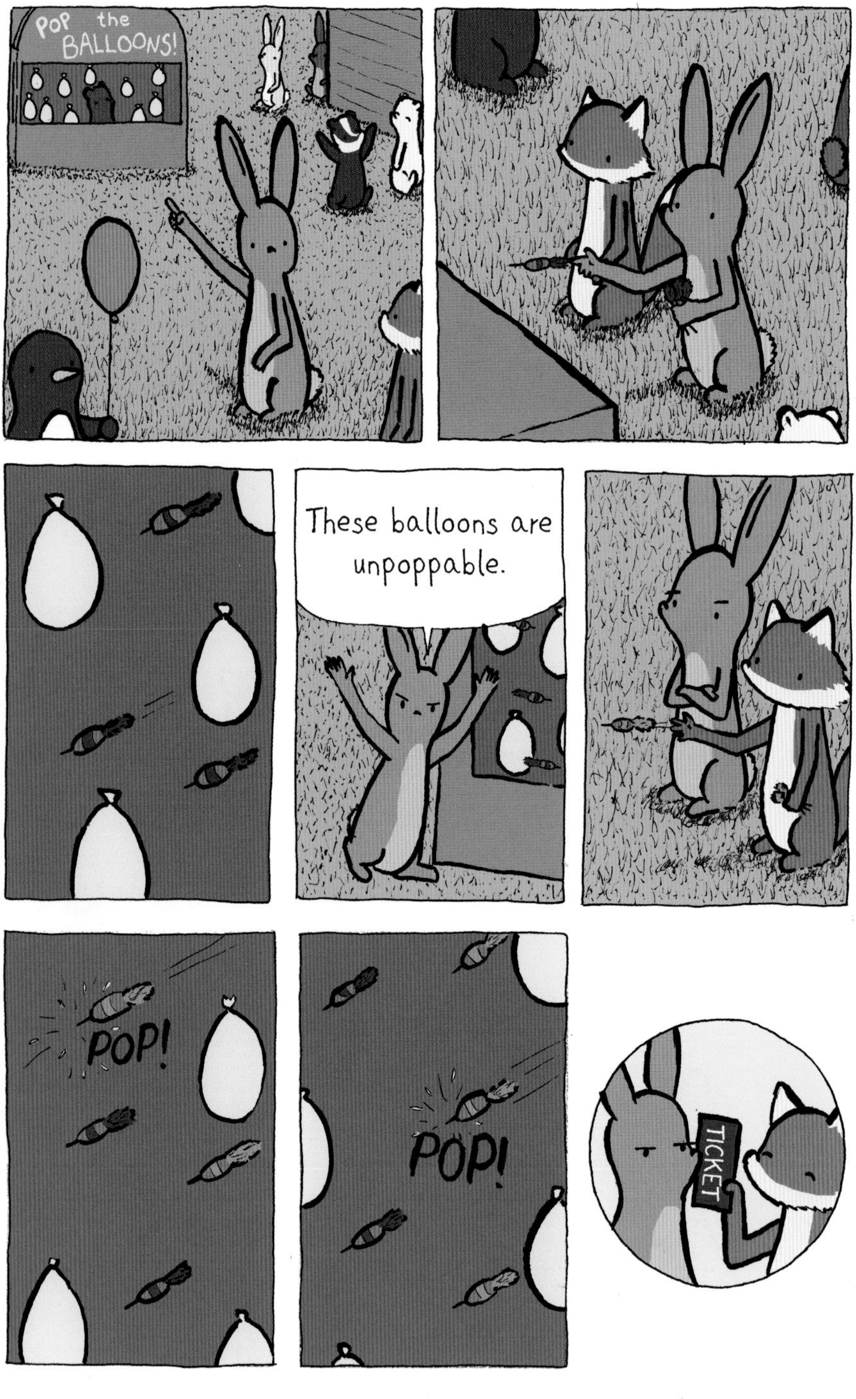
POP the BALLOONS!
These balloons are unpoppable.
POP!
POP!
TICKET

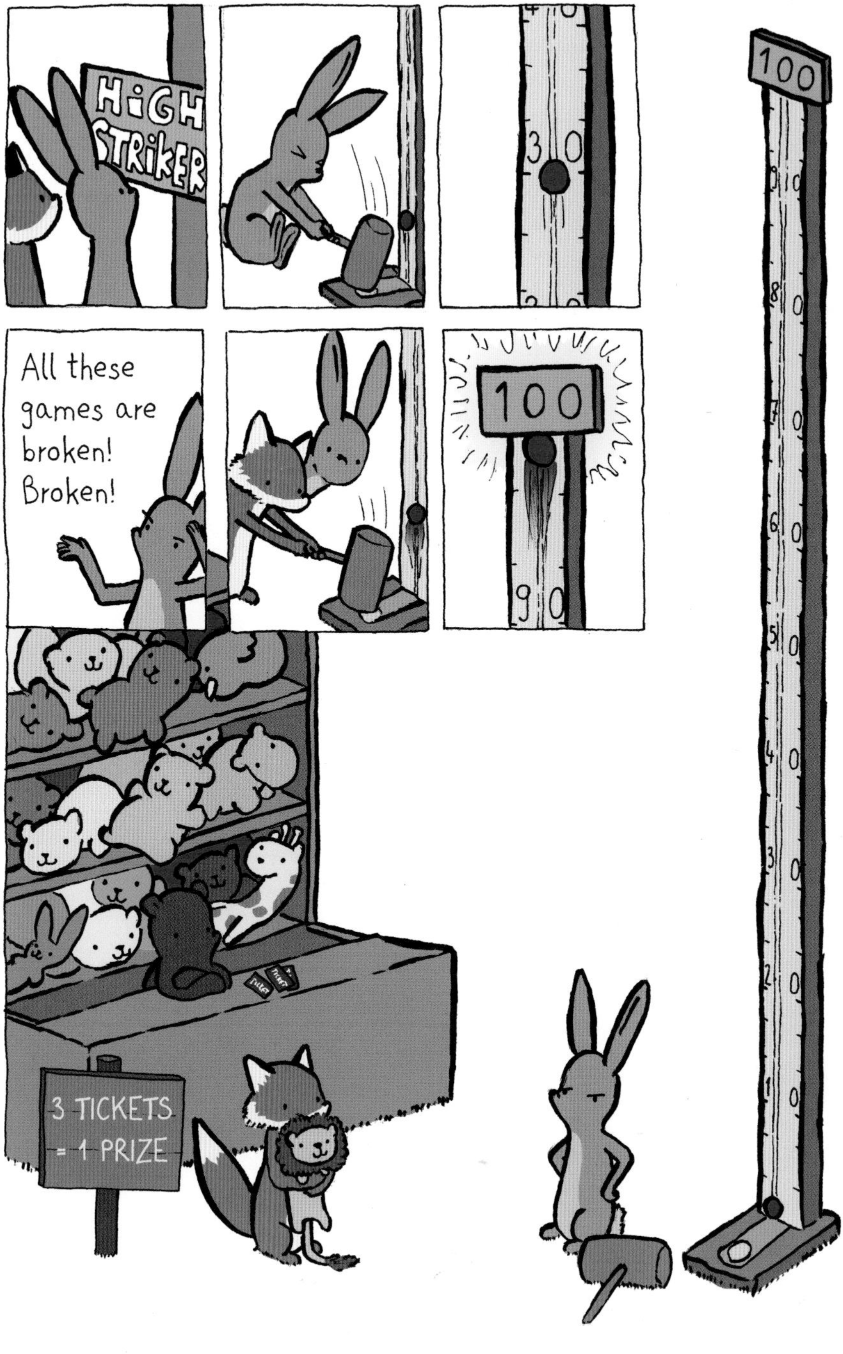
HiGH STRiKER
All these games are broken! Broken!
100
3 TICKETS = 1 PRIZE
100

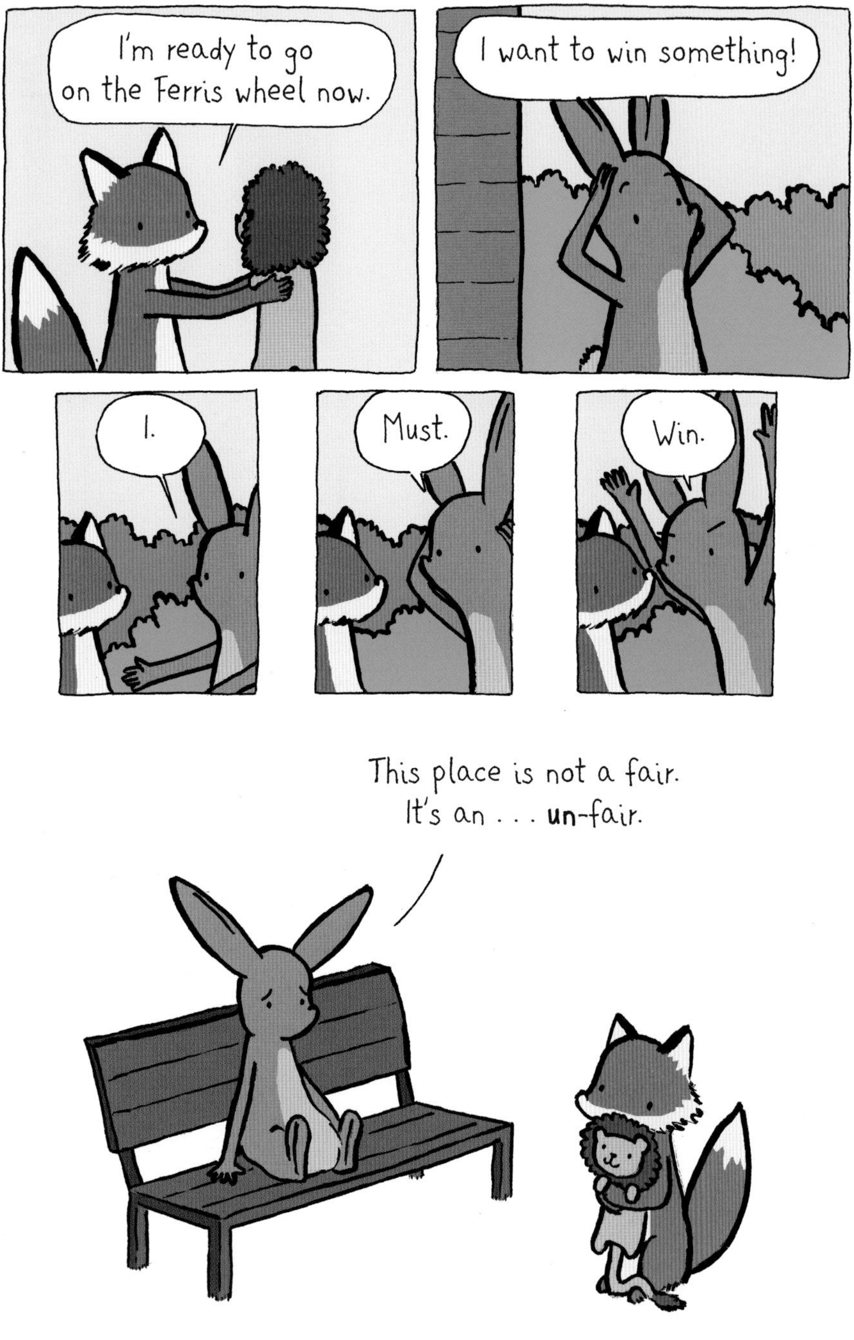
I'm ready to go on the Ferris wheel now.
I want to win something!
I.
Must.
Win.
This place is not a fair. It's an . . . **un**-fair.

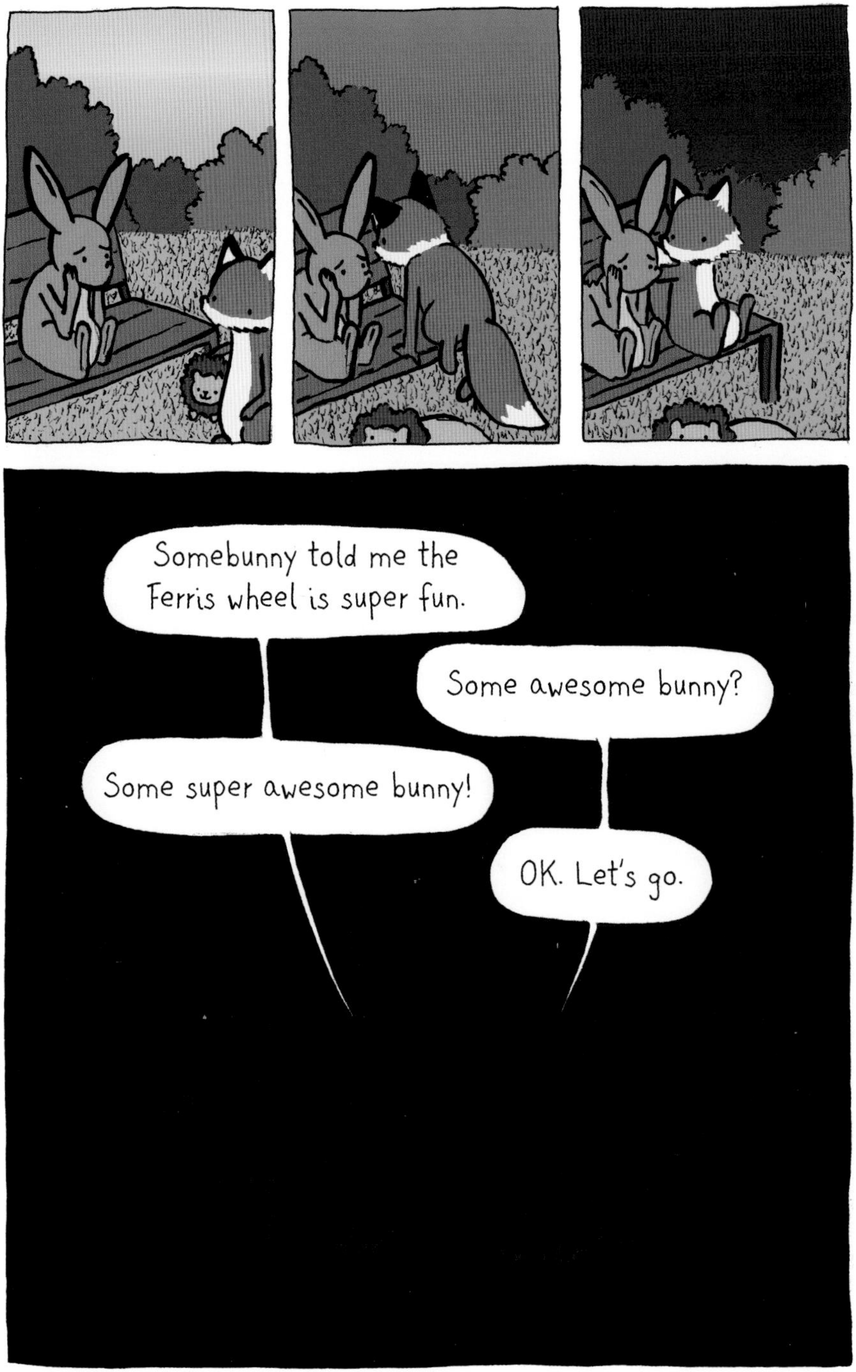
Somebunny told me the Ferris wheel is super fun.
Some awesome bunny?
Some super awesome bunny!
OK. Let's go.

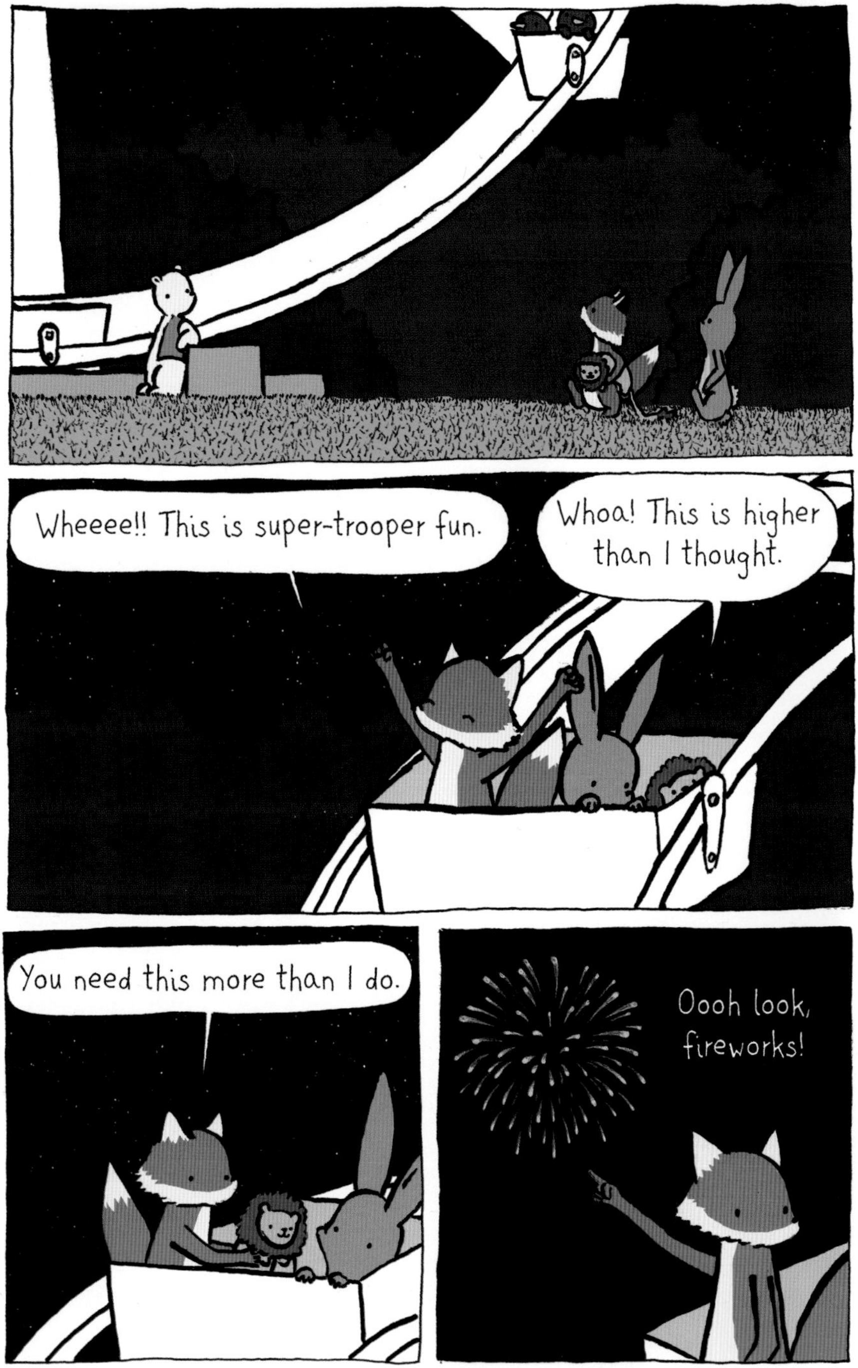
Wheeee!! This is super-trooper fun.
Whoa! This is higher than I thought.
You need this more than I do.
Oooh look, fireworks!

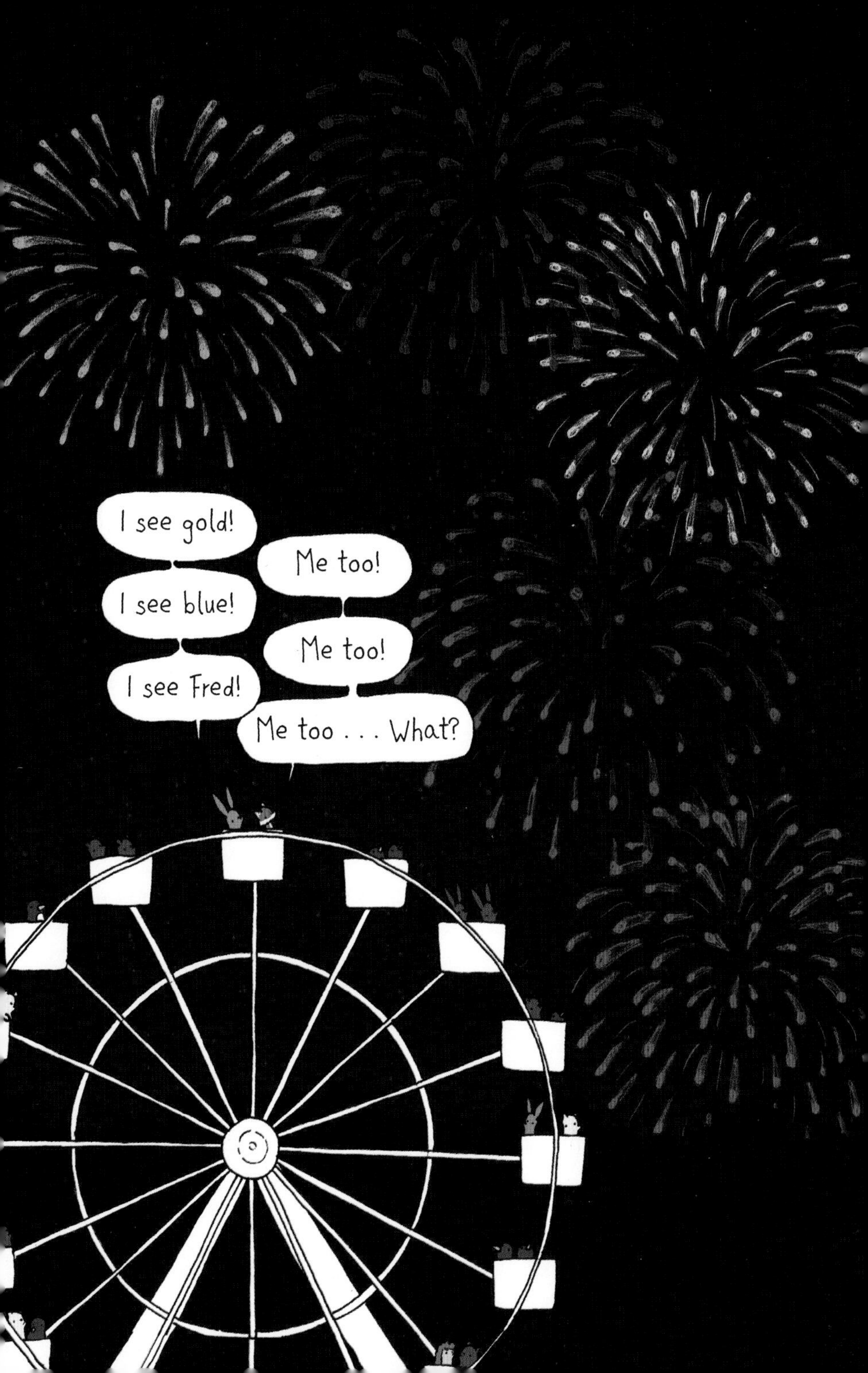
I see gold!
Me too!
I see blue!
Me too!
I see Fred!
Me too . . . What?

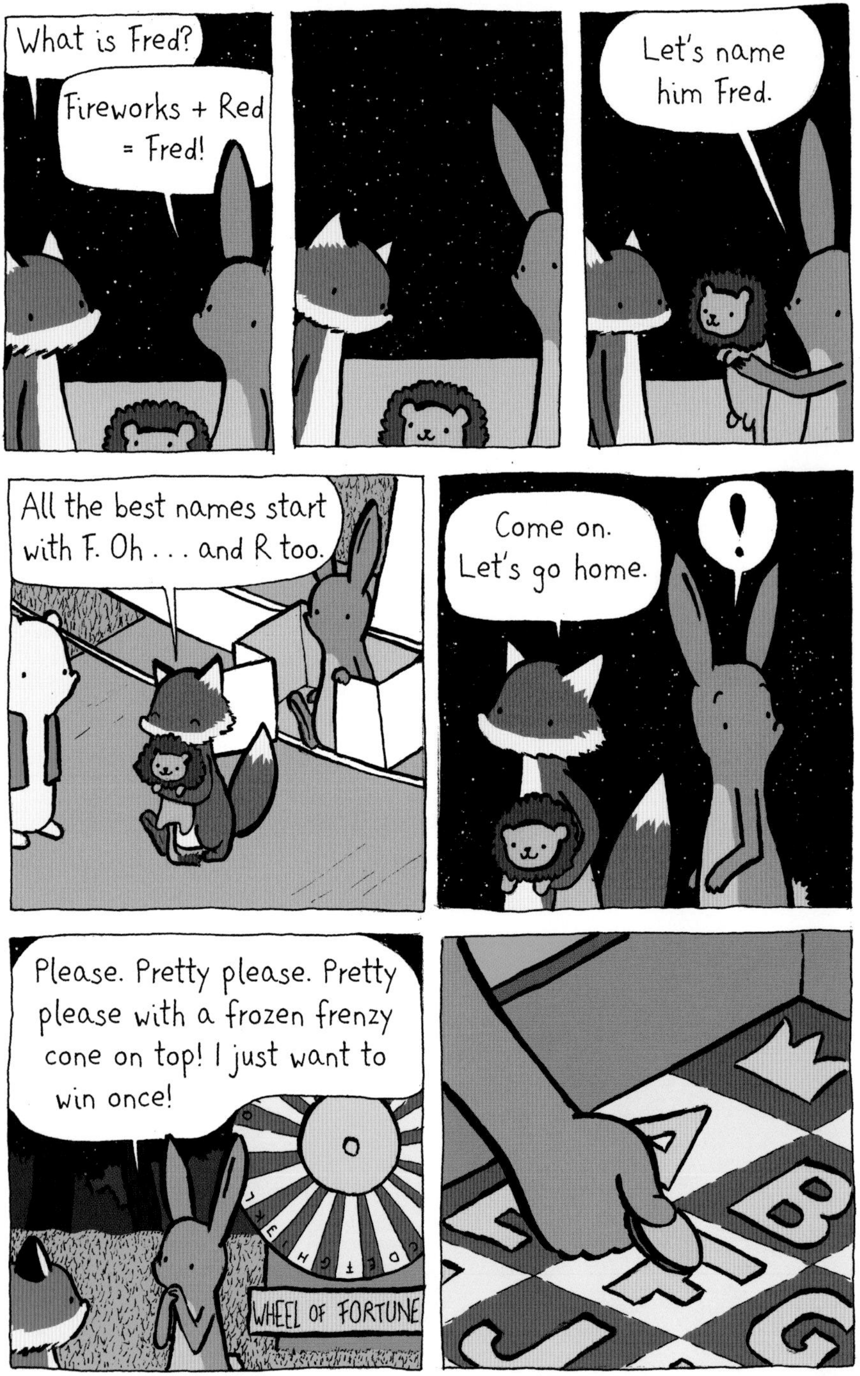
What is Fred?
Fireworks + Red = Fred!
Let's name him Fred.
All the best names start with F. Oh . . . and R too.
Come on. Let's go home.
!
Please. Pretty please. Pretty please with a frozen frenzy cone on top! I just want to win once!
WHEEL OF FORTUNE

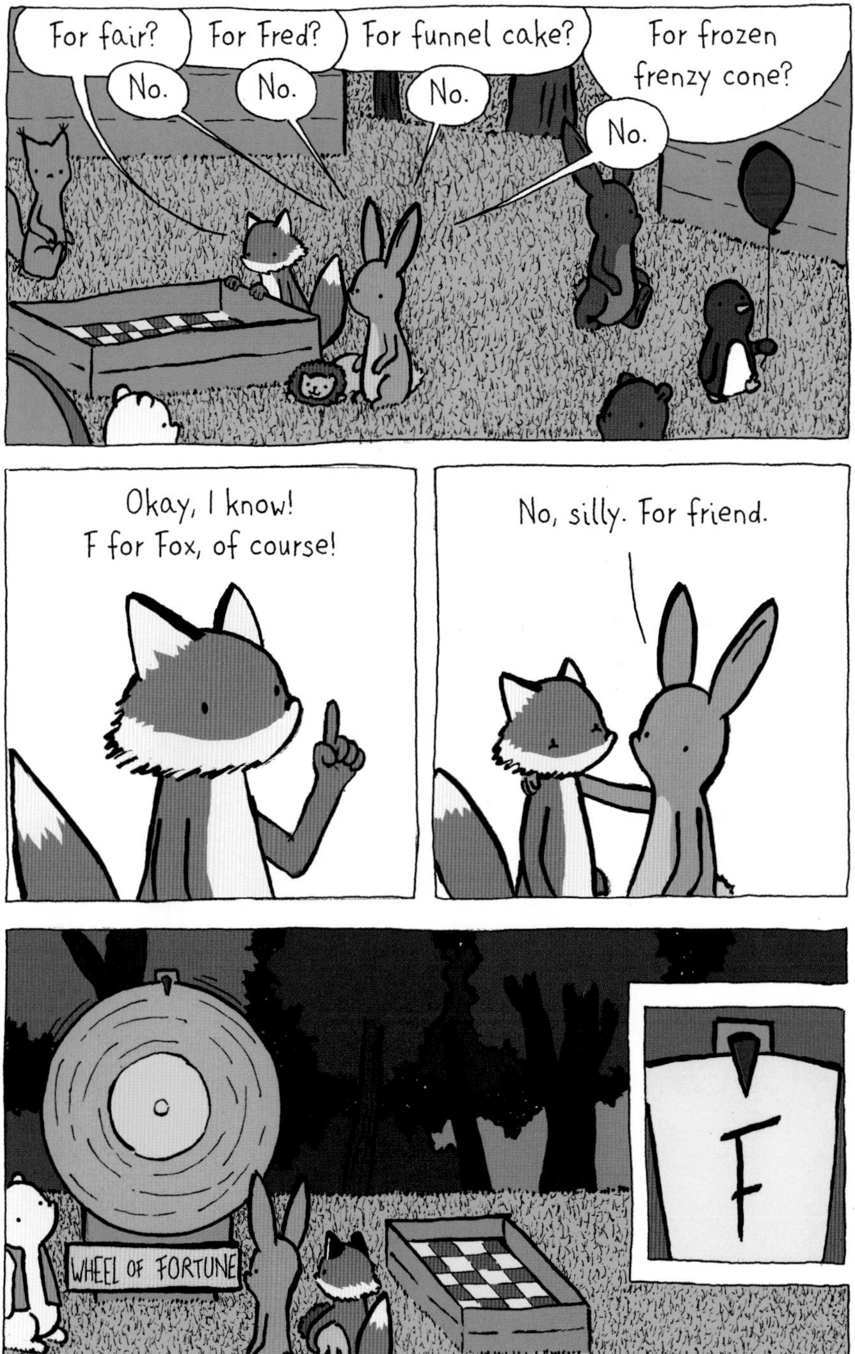
For fair?
No.
For Fred?
No.
For funnel cake?
No.
For frozen frenzy cone?
No.
Okay, I know! F for Fox, of course!
No, silly. For friend.
WHEEL OF FORTUNE
F

I won! I won! I'm a winner! I'm a spinner! I'm a
spinner winner! I'm a super duper loop-the-looper
cotton candy dinner winner. I'm a . . .

Stop! The whole fair
knows you're a winner.

What'd I win?

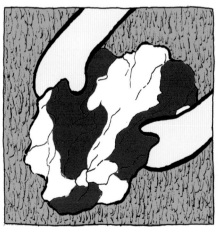

Plastic? Plastic? I won a lousy
piece of plastic? No fair!

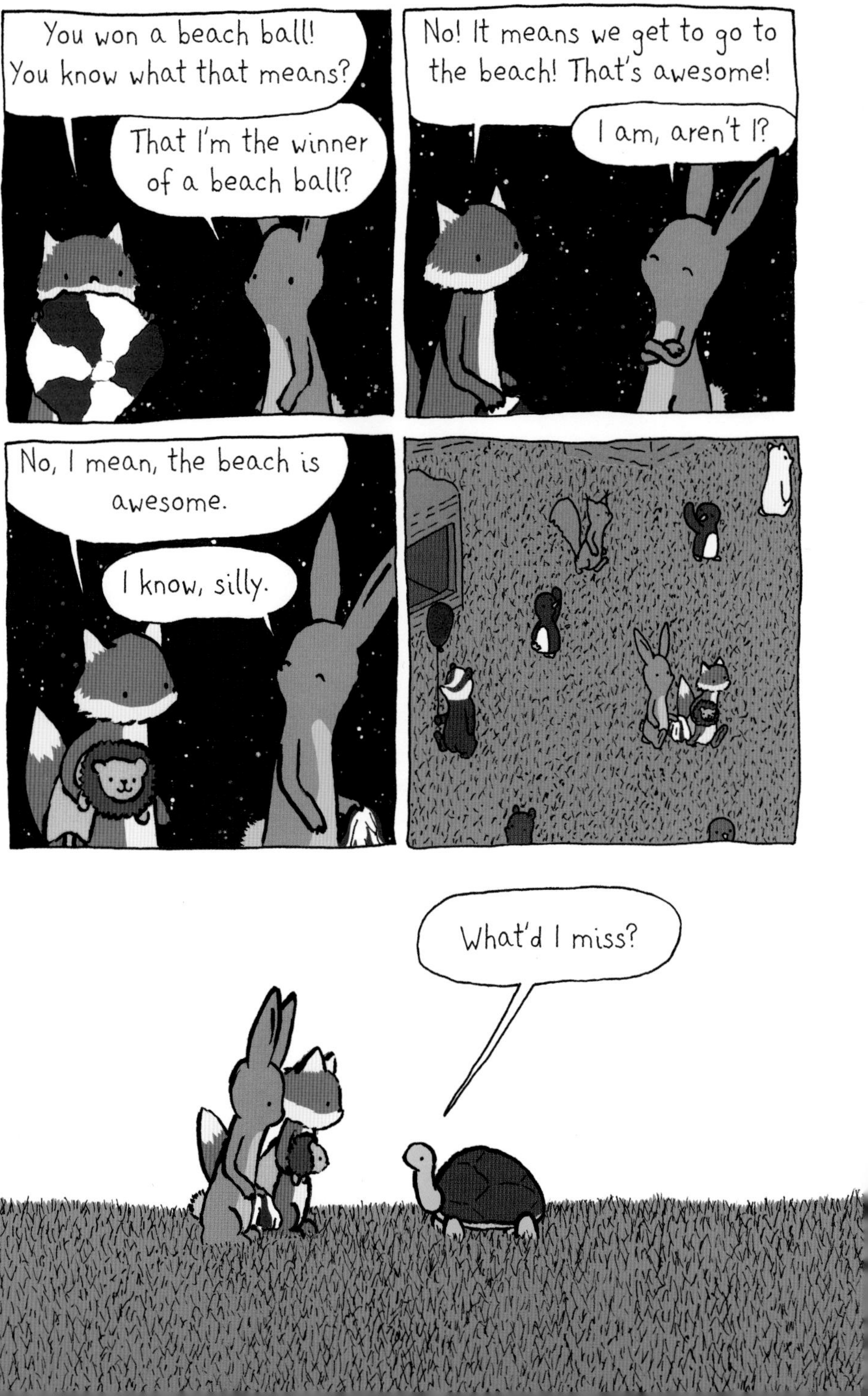
You won a beach ball! You know what that means?
That I'm the winner of a beach ball?
No! It means we get to go to the beach! That's awesome!
I am, aren't I?
No, I mean, the beach is awesome.
I know, silly.
What'd I miss?

STORY TWO

SAND, SWIMMING & SUNSET

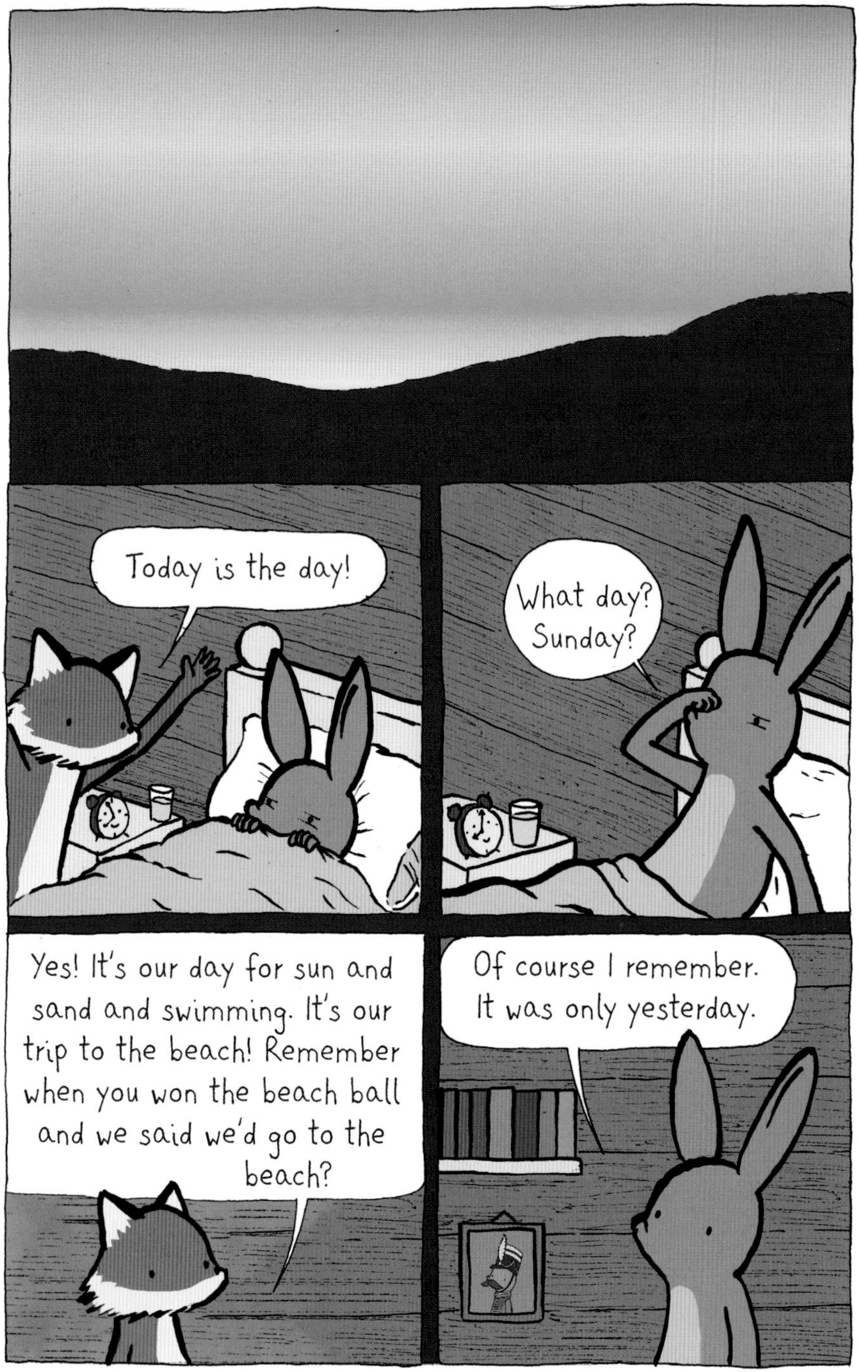
Today is the day!
What day? Sunday?
Yes! It's our day for sun and sand and swimming. It's our trip to the beach! Remember when you won the beach ball and we said we'd go to the beach?
Of course I remember. It was only yesterday.

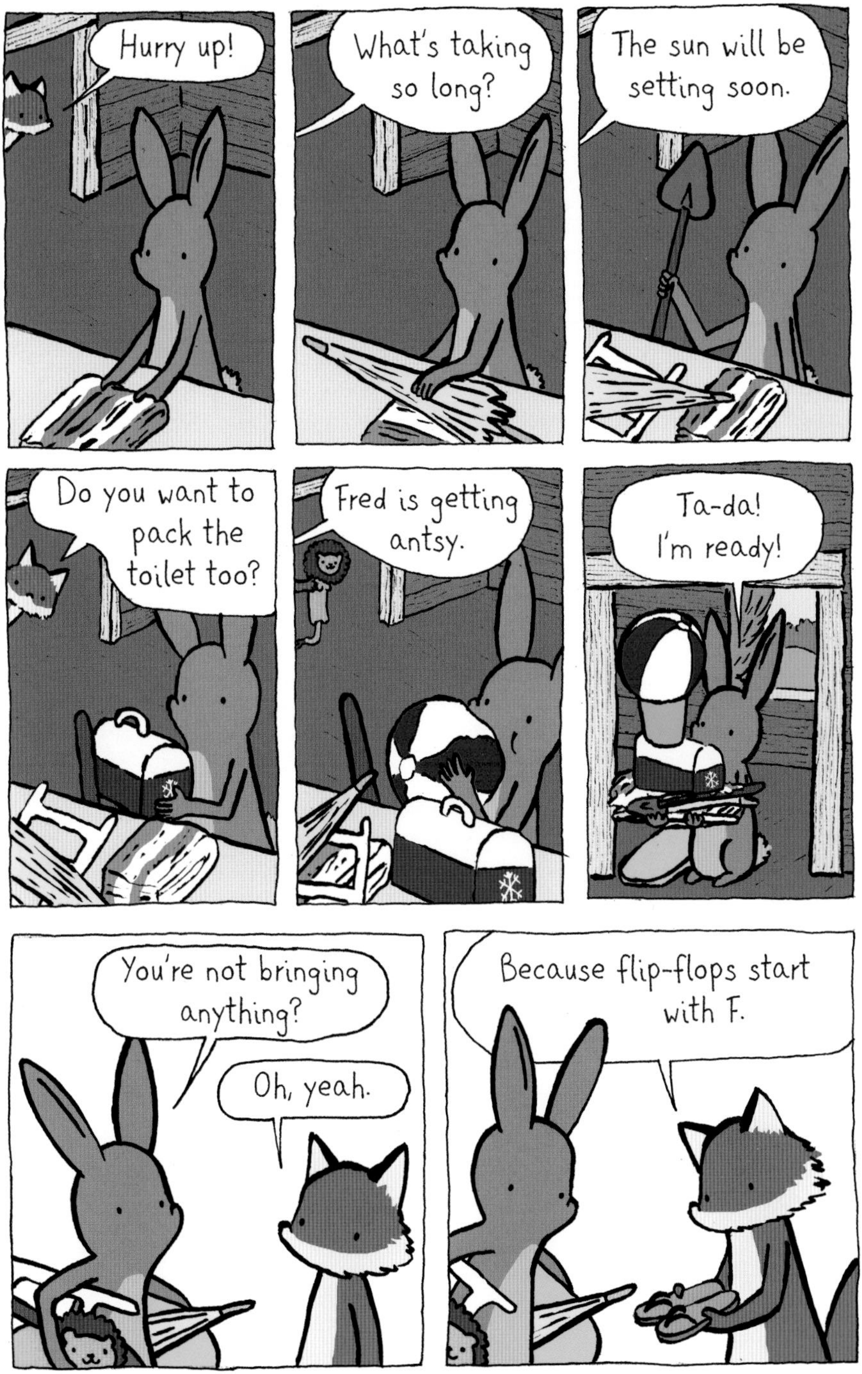
Hurry up!
What's taking so long?
The sun will be setting soon.
Do you want to pack the toilet too?
Fred is getting antsy.
Ta-da! I'm ready!
You're not bringing anything?
Oh, yeah.
Because flip-flops start with F.

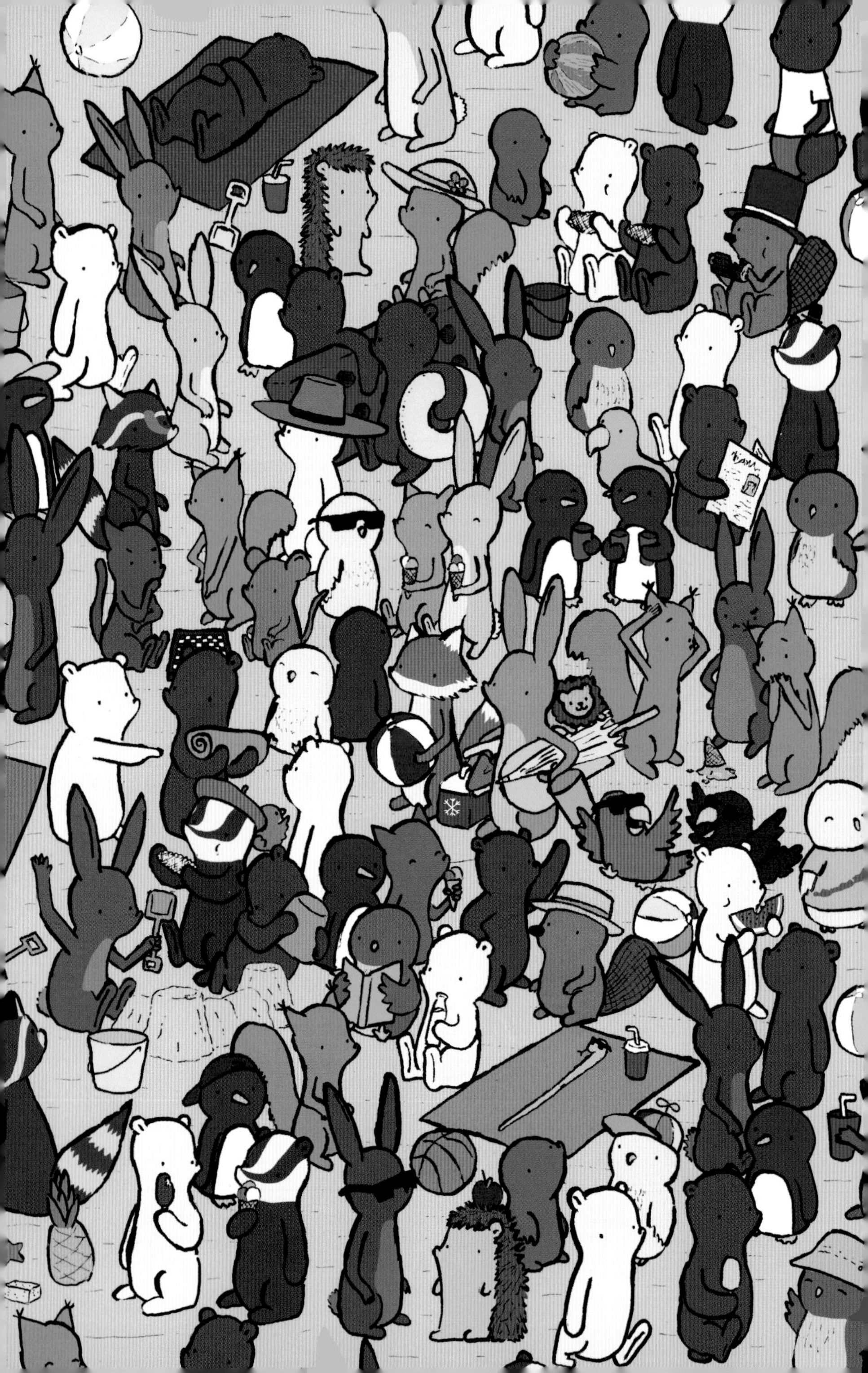

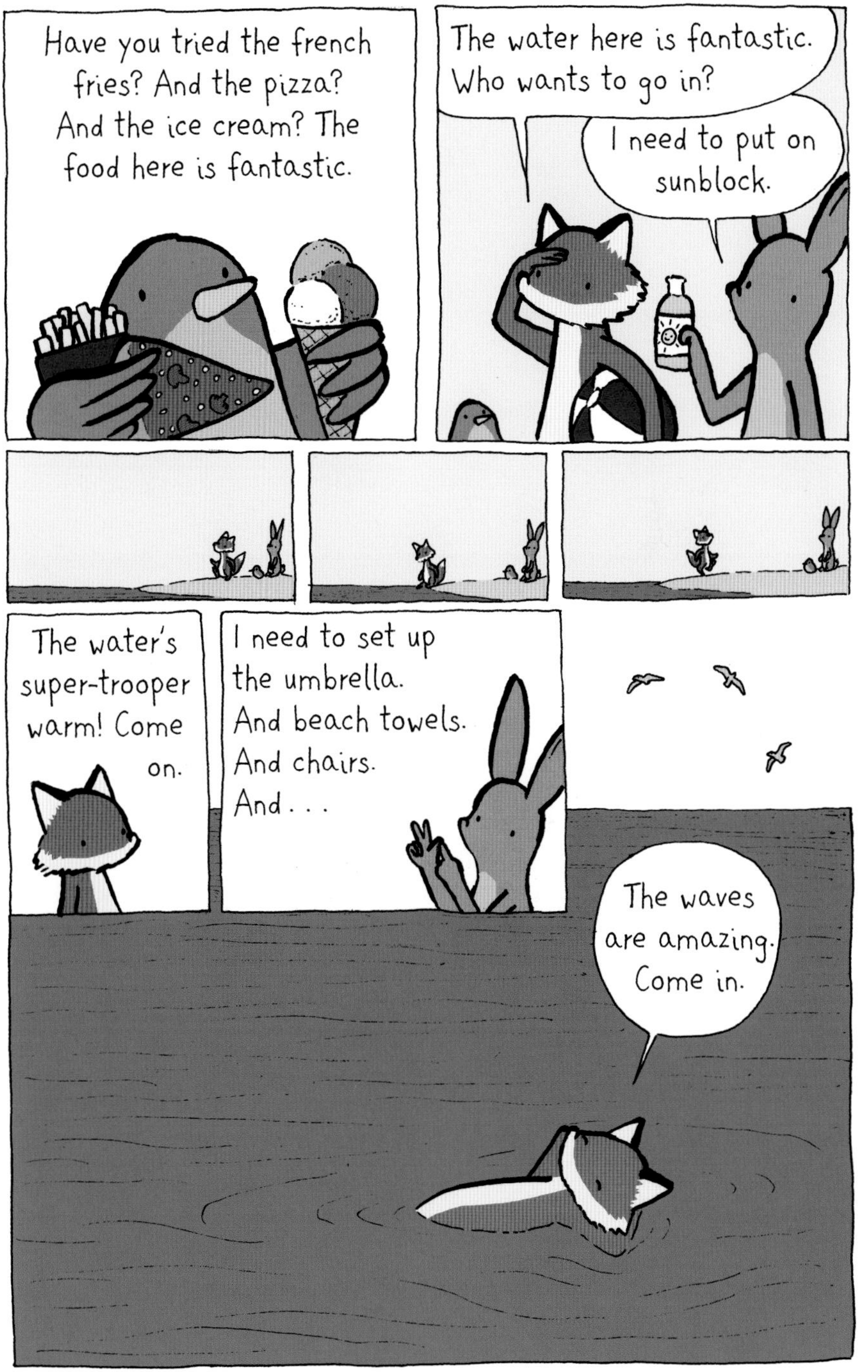
Have you tried the french fries? And the pizza? And the ice cream? The food here is fantastic.
The water here is fantastic. Who wants to go in?
I need to put on sunblock.
The water's super-trooper warm! Come on.
I need to set up the umbrella. And beach towels. And chairs. And . . .
The waves are amazing. Come in.

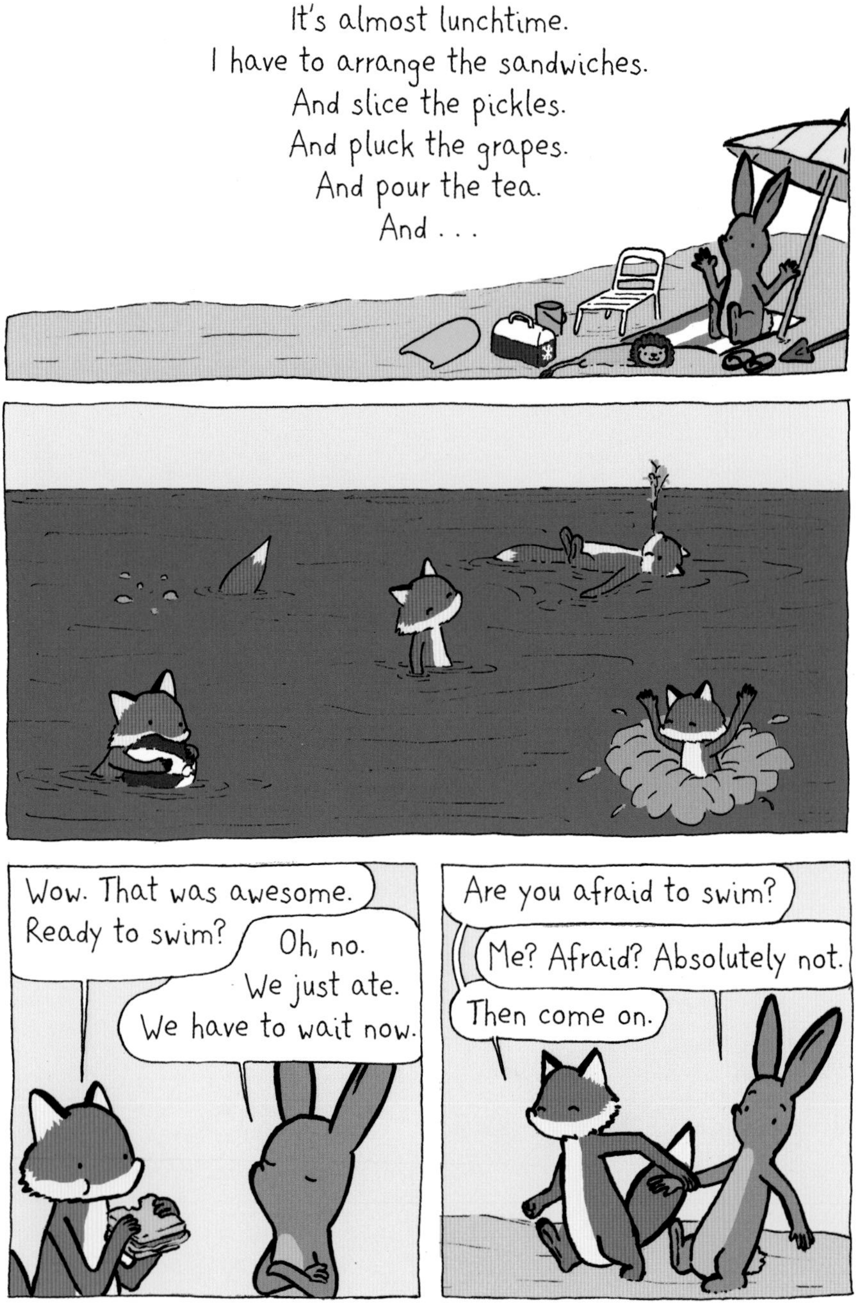
It's almost lunchtime.
I have to arrange the sandwiches.
And slice the pickles.
And pluck the grapes.
And pour the tea.
And . . .
Wow. That was awesome.
Ready to swim?
Oh, no.
We just ate.
We have to wait now.
Are you afraid to swim?
Me? Afraid? Absolutely not.
Then come on.

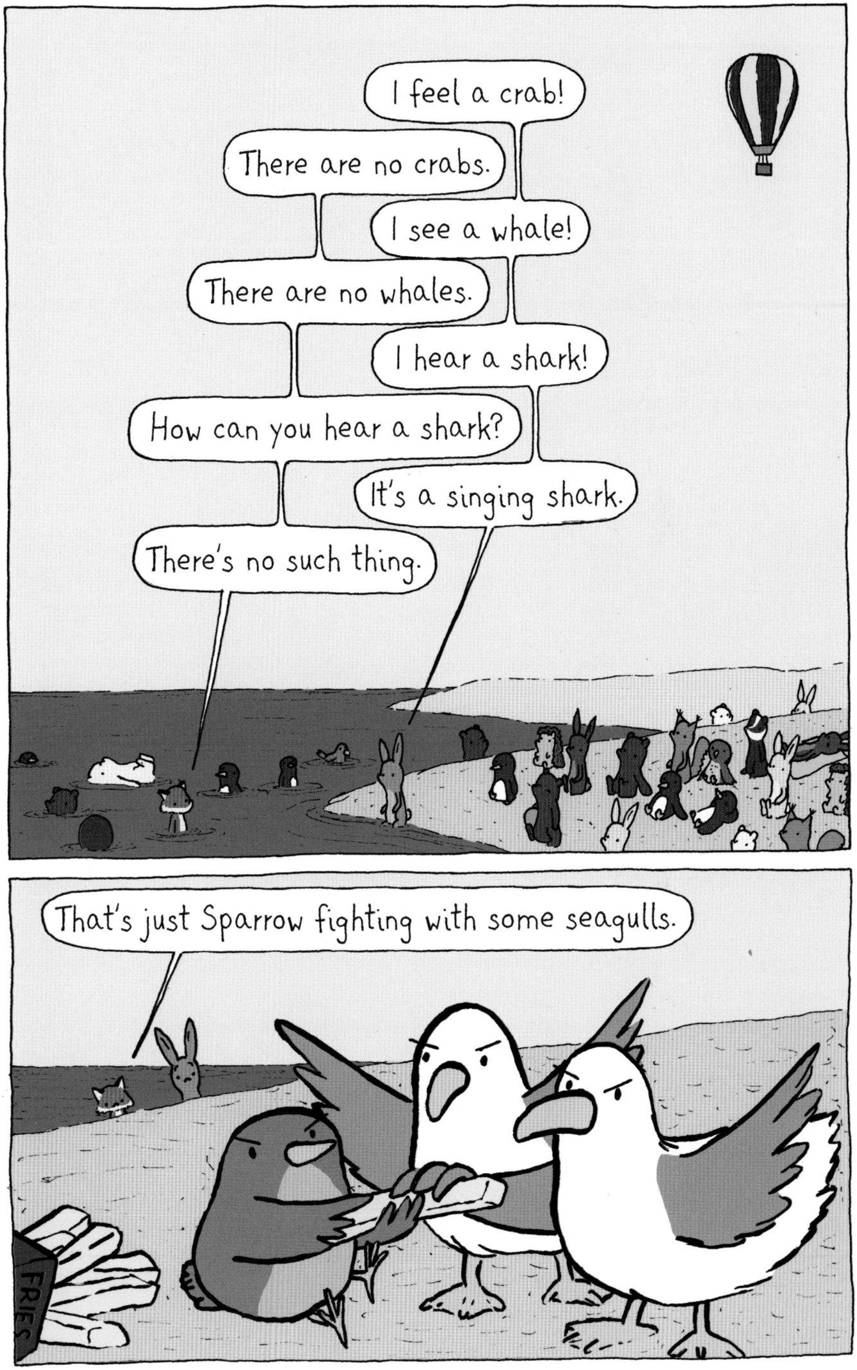
I feel a crab!
There are no crabs.
I see a whale!
There are no whales.
I hear a shark!
How can you hear a shark?
It's a singing shark.
There's no such thing.
That's just Sparrow fighting with some seagulls.
FRIES

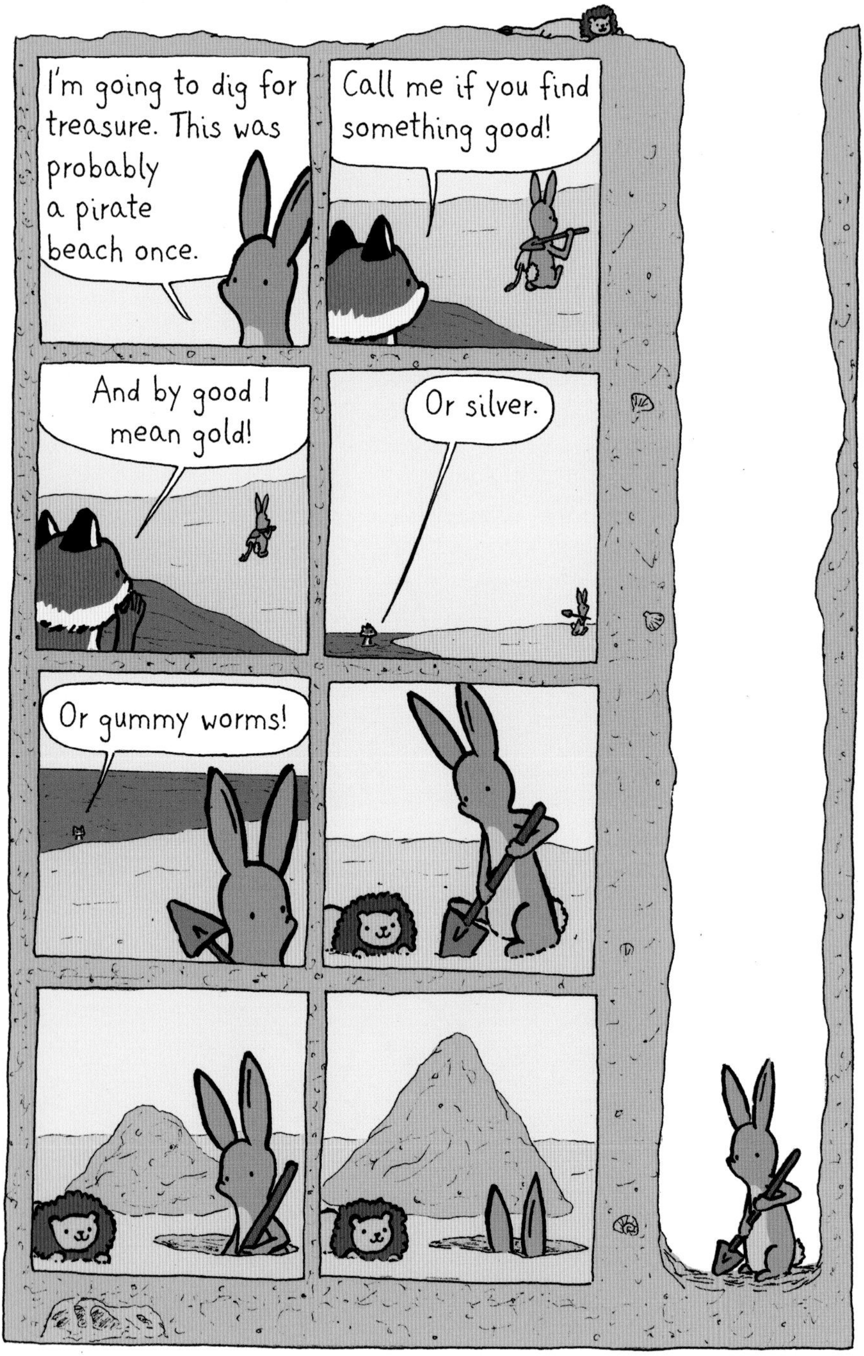
I'm going to dig for treasure. This was probably a pirate beach once.
Call me if you find something good!
And by good I mean gold!
Or silver.
Or gummy worms!

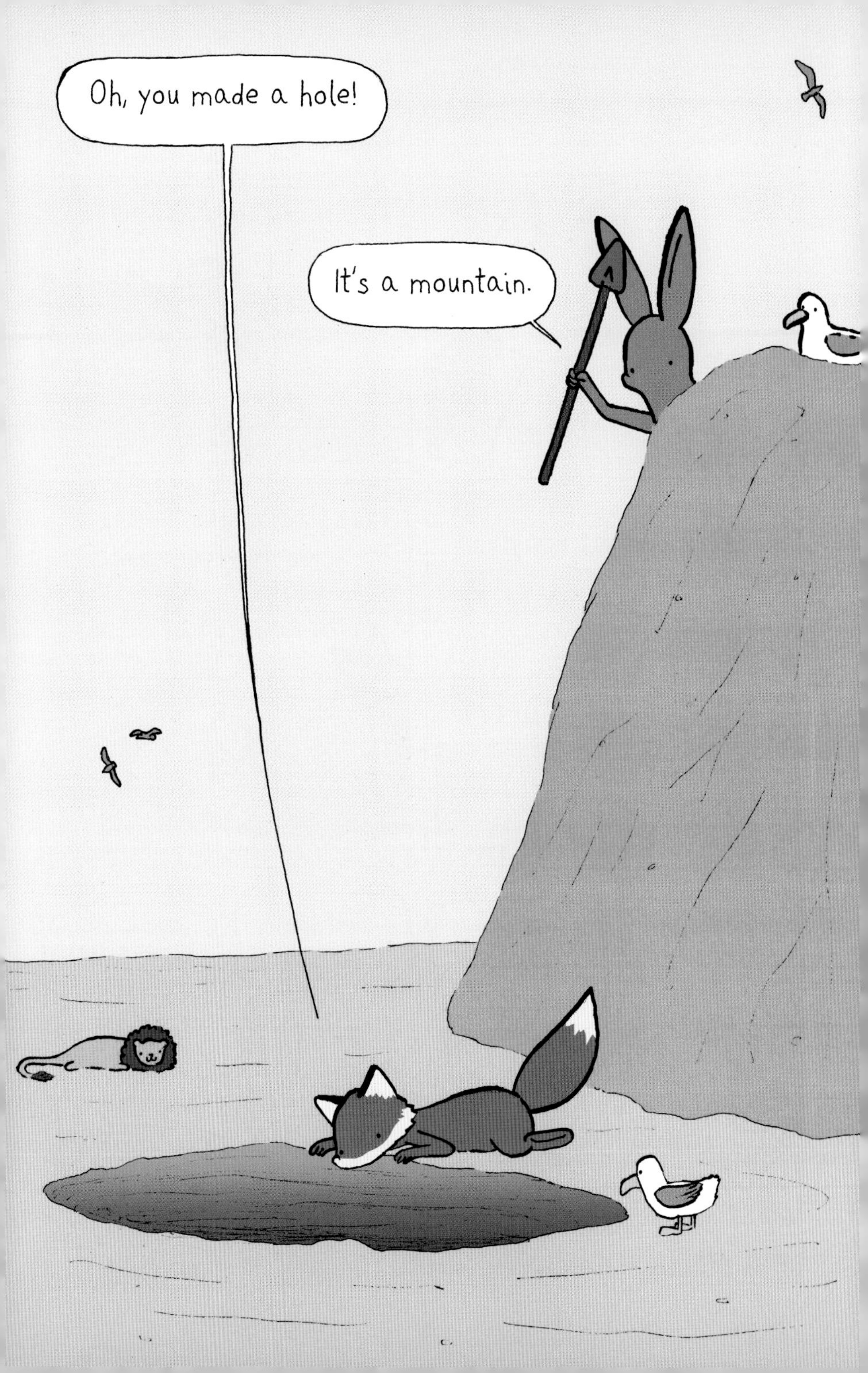
Oh, you made a hole!
It's a mountain.

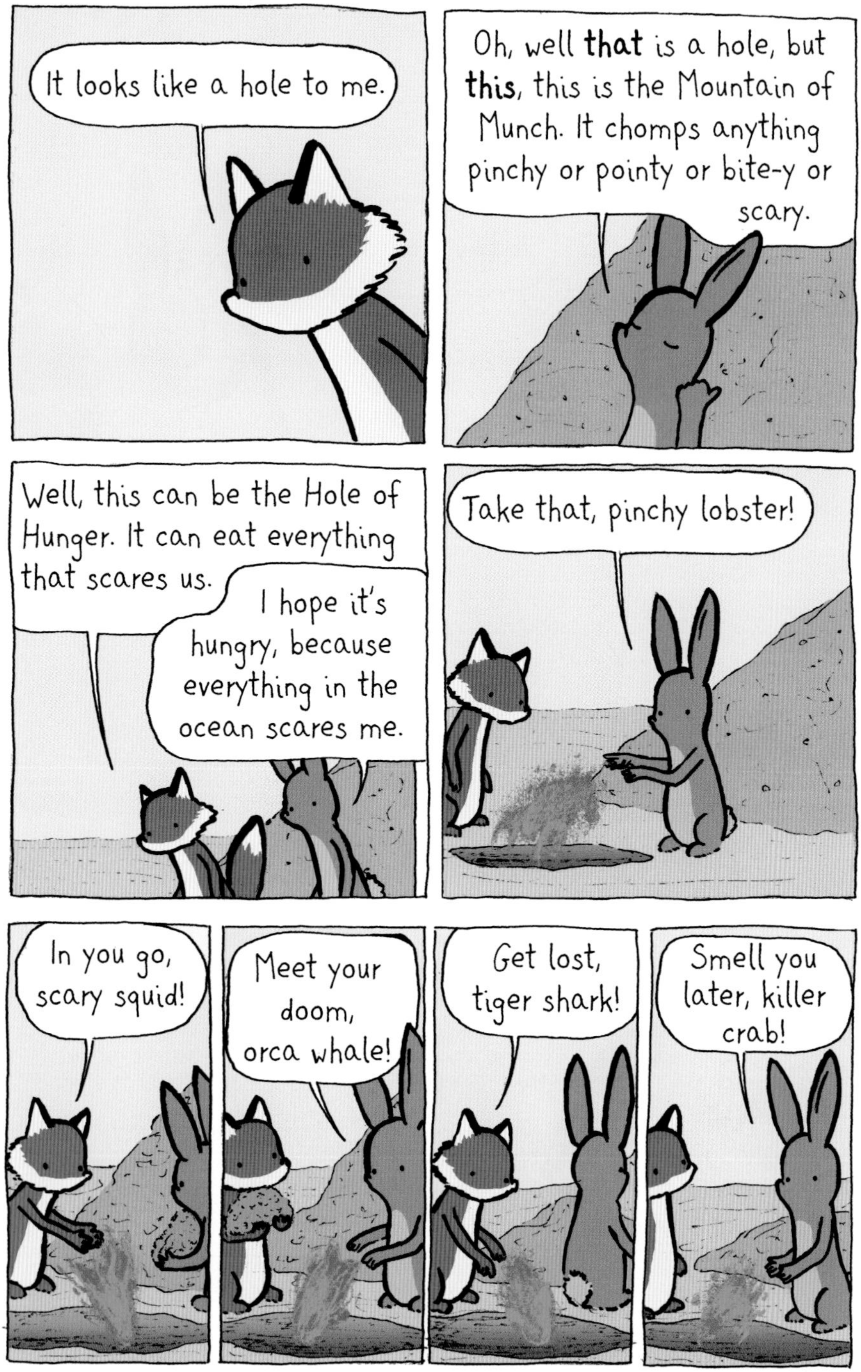
It looks like a hole to me.
Oh, well **that** is a hole, but **this**, this is the Mountain of Munch. It chomps anything pinchy or pointy or bite-y or scary.
Well, this can be the Hole of Hunger. It can eat everything that scares us.
I hope it's hungry, because everything in the ocean scares me.
Take that, pinchy lobster!
In you go, scary squid!
Meet your doom, orca whale!
Get lost, tiger shark!
Smell you later, killer crab!

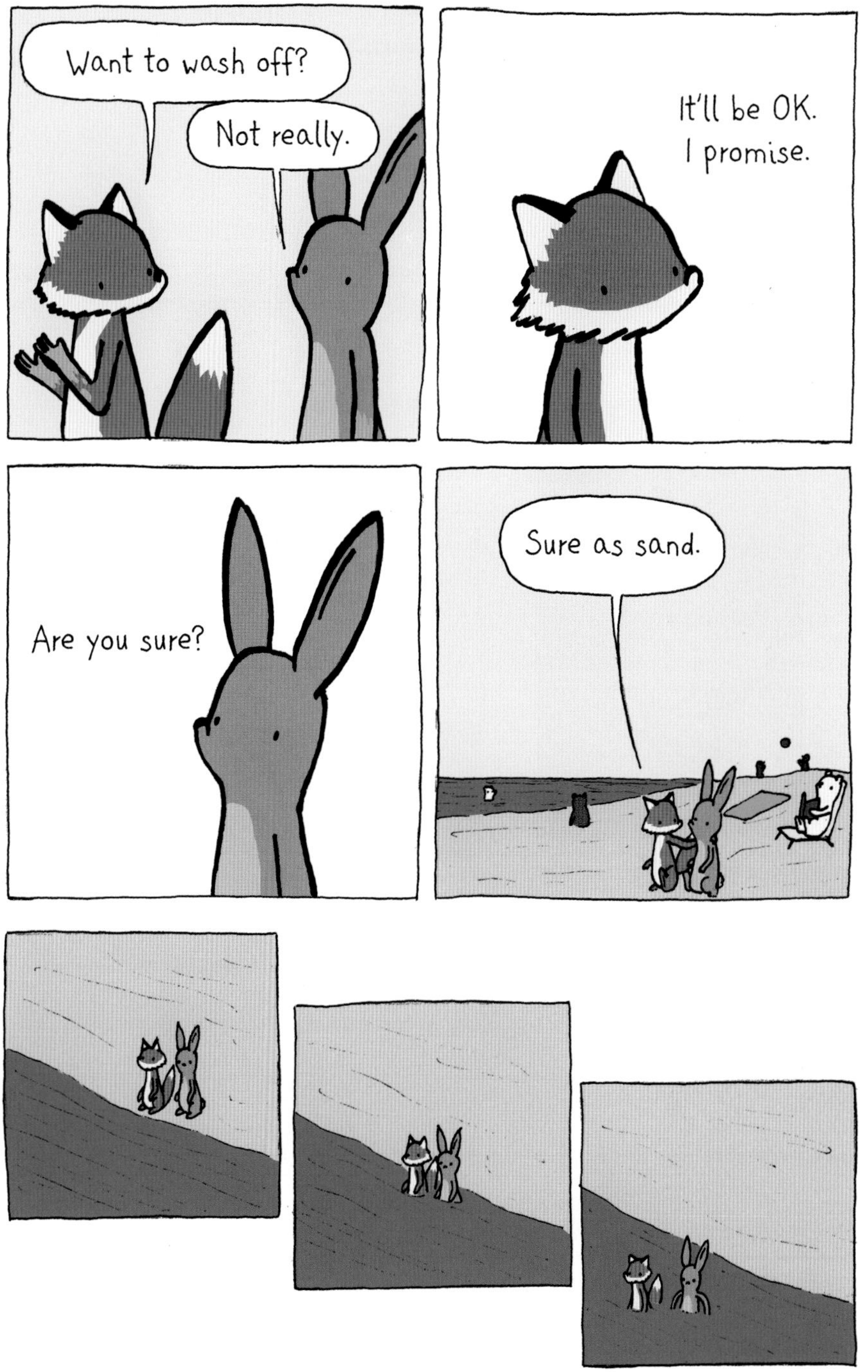
Want to wash off?
Not really.
It'll be OK.
I promise.
Are you sure?
Sure as sand.

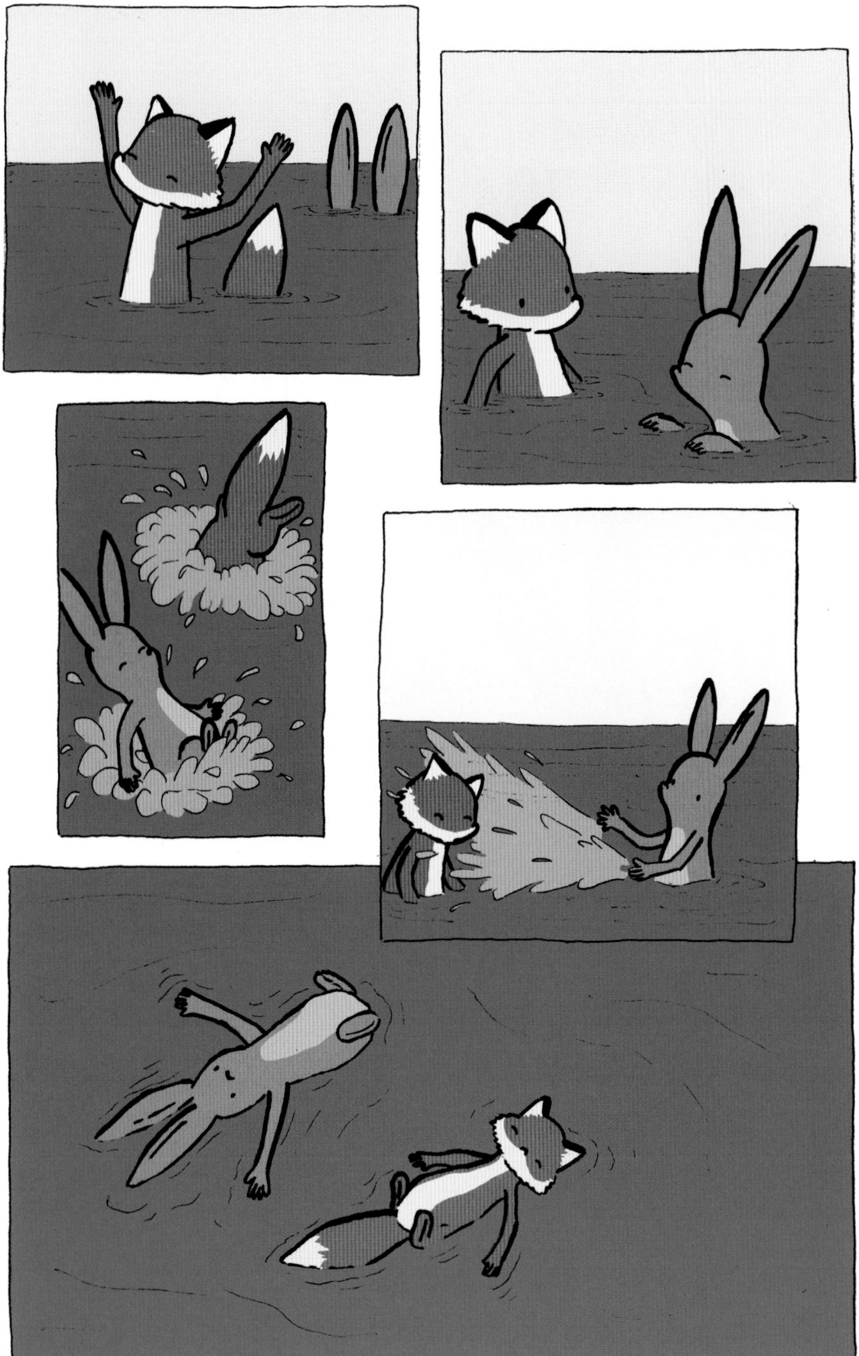

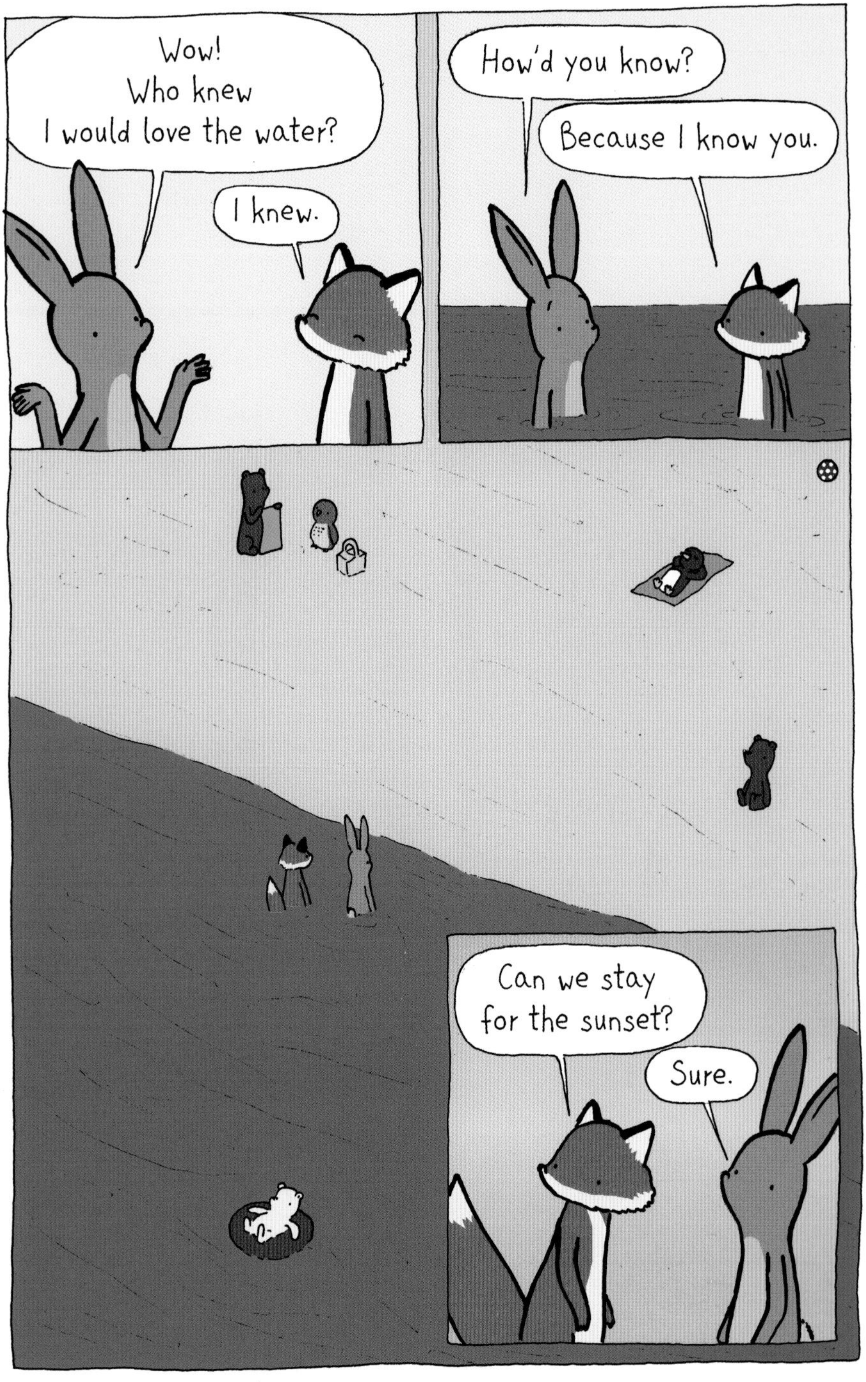
Wow! Who knew I would love the water?
I knew.
How'd you know?
Because I know you.
Can we stay for the sunset?
Sure.

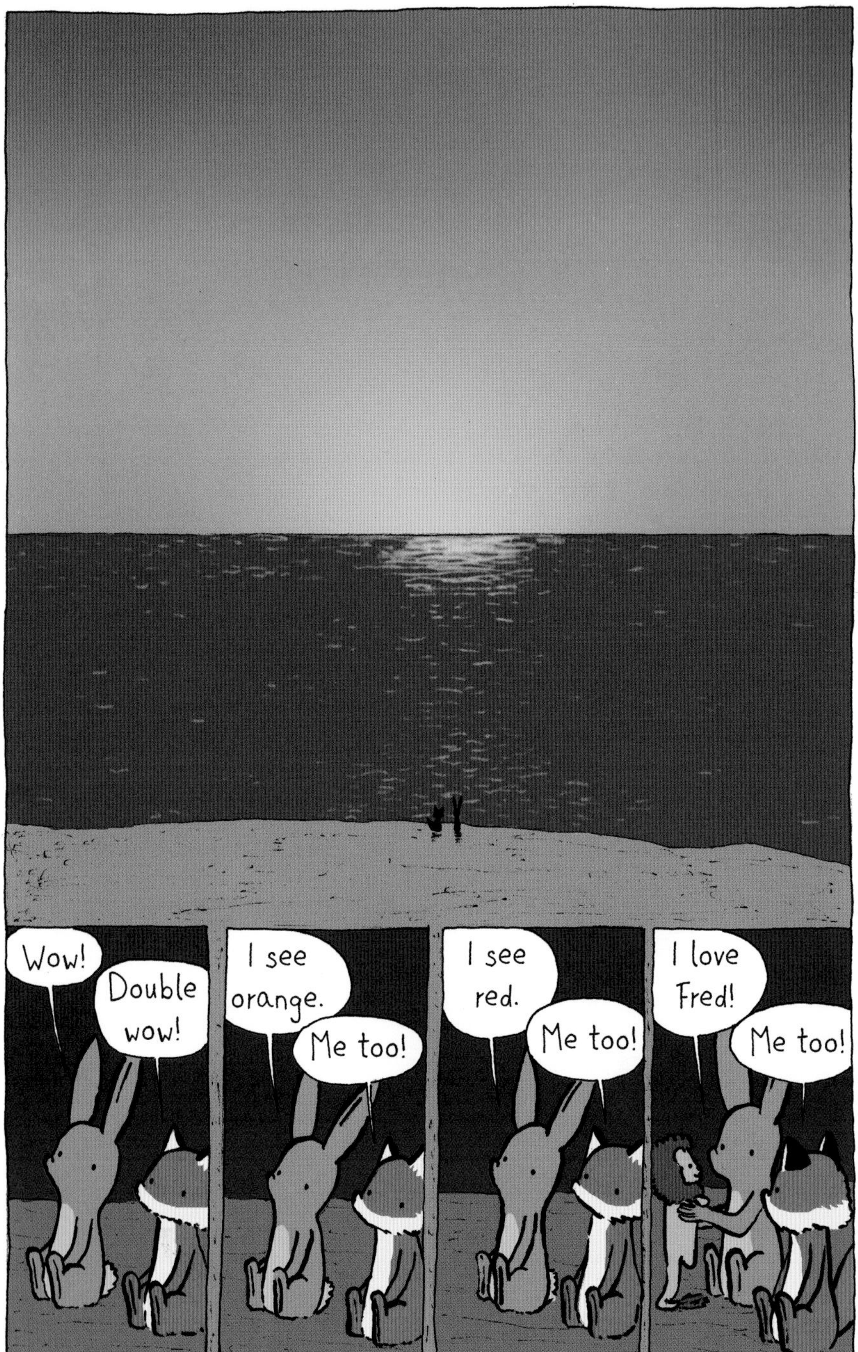
Wow!
Double wow!
I see orange.
Me too!
I see red.
Me too!
I love Fred!
Me too!

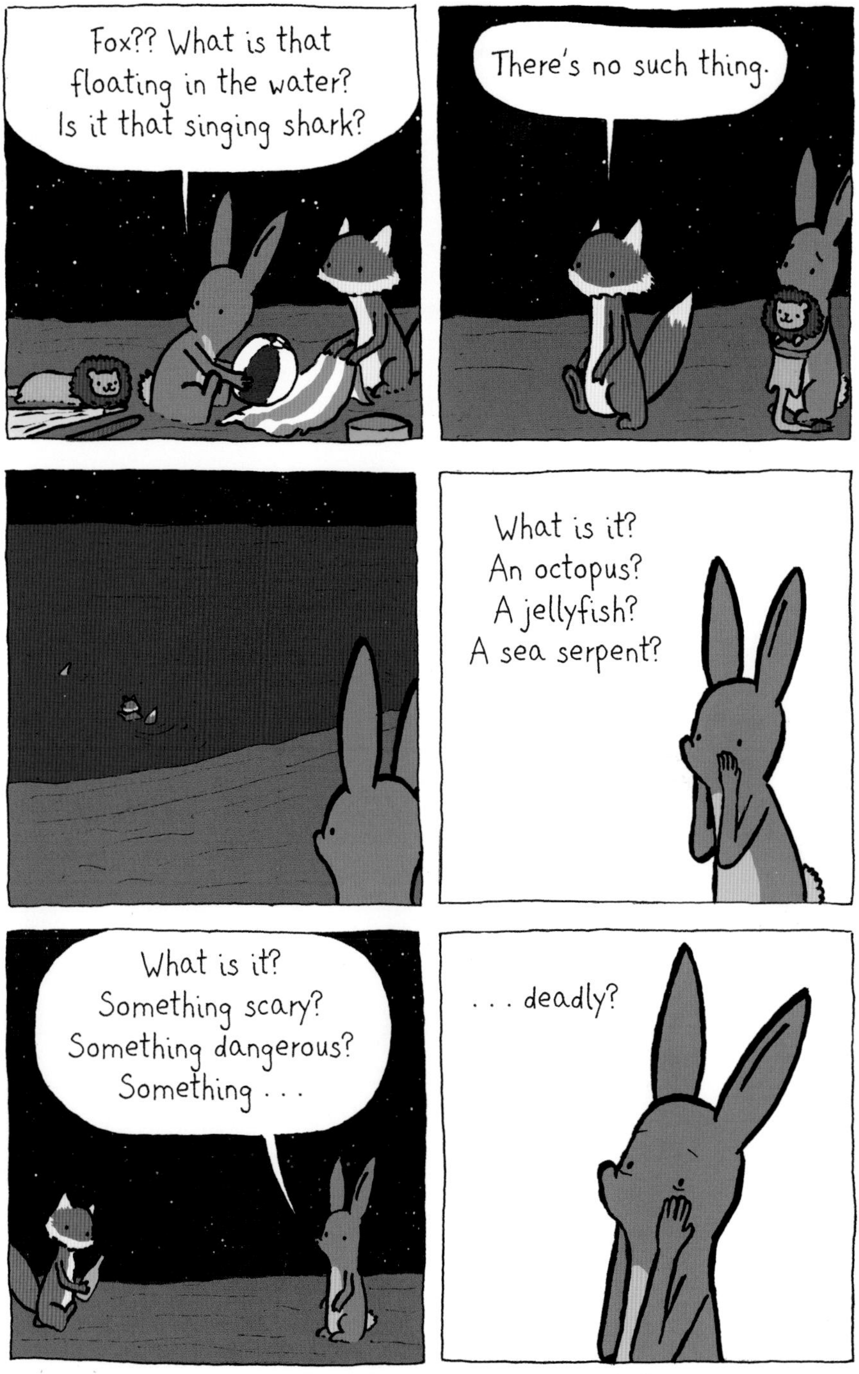
Fox?? What is that floating in the water? Is it that singing shark?
There's no such thing.
What is it?
An octopus?
A jellyfish?
A sea serpent?
What is it?
Something scary?
Something dangerous?
Something . . .
. . . deadly?

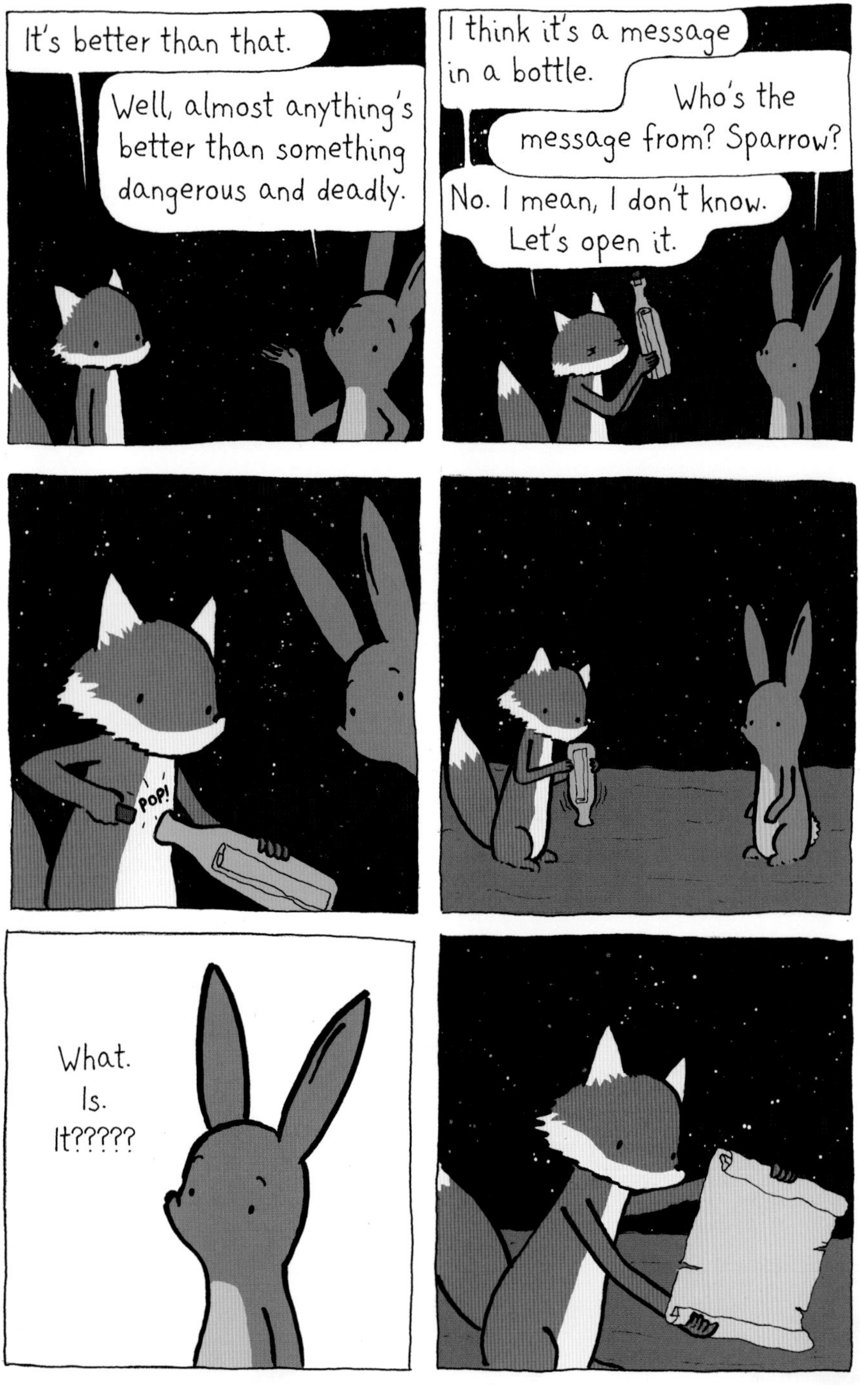
It's better than that.
Well, almost anything's better than something dangerous and deadly.
I think it's a message in a bottle.
Who's the message from? Sparrow?
No. I mean, I don't know. Let's open it.
POP!
What.
Is.
It?????

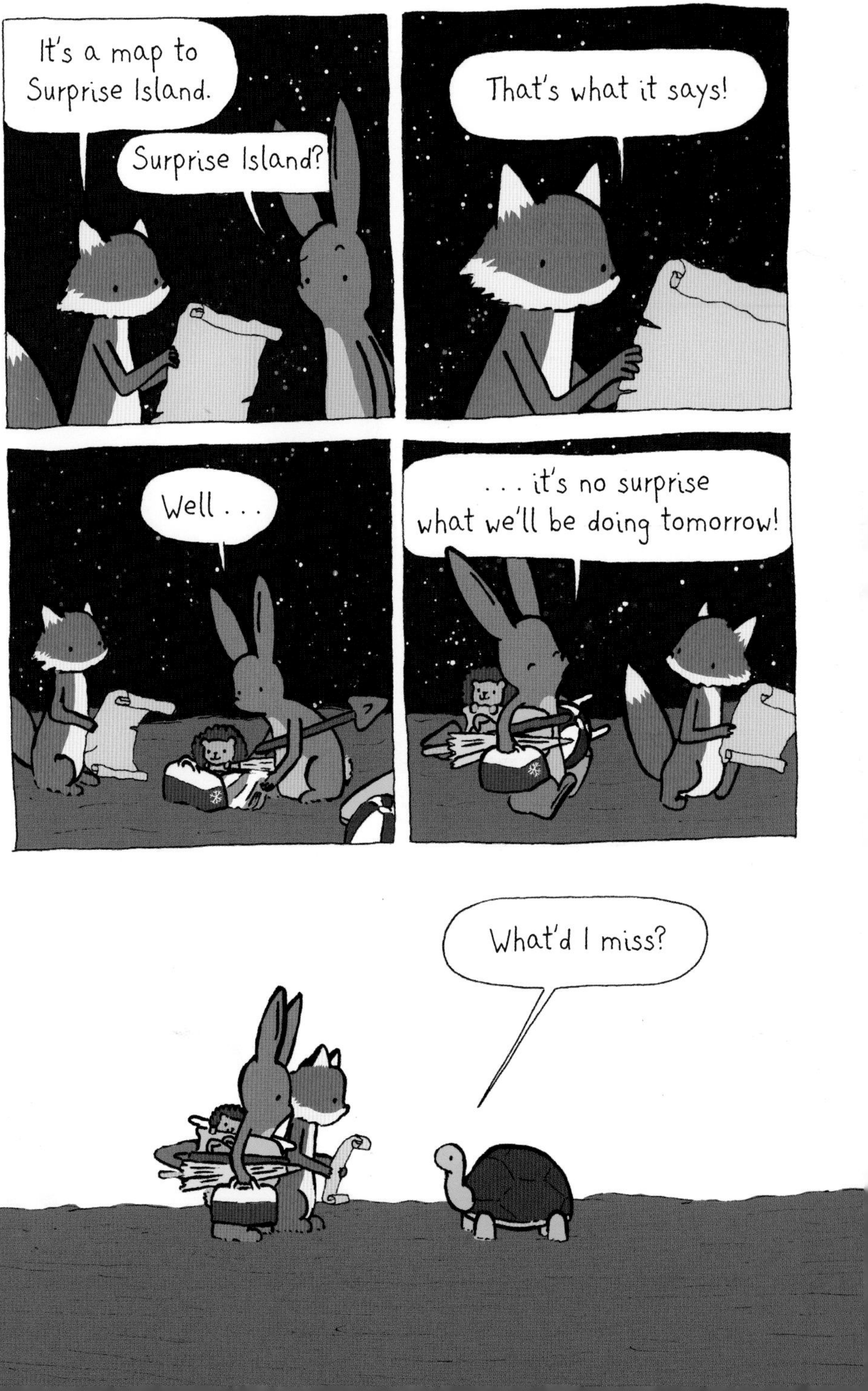
It's a map to Surprise Island.
Surprise Island?
That's what it says!
Well . . .
. . . it's no surprise what we'll be doing tomorrow!
What'd I miss?

STORY THREE

SURPRISES, SWAMPS & SEEDS

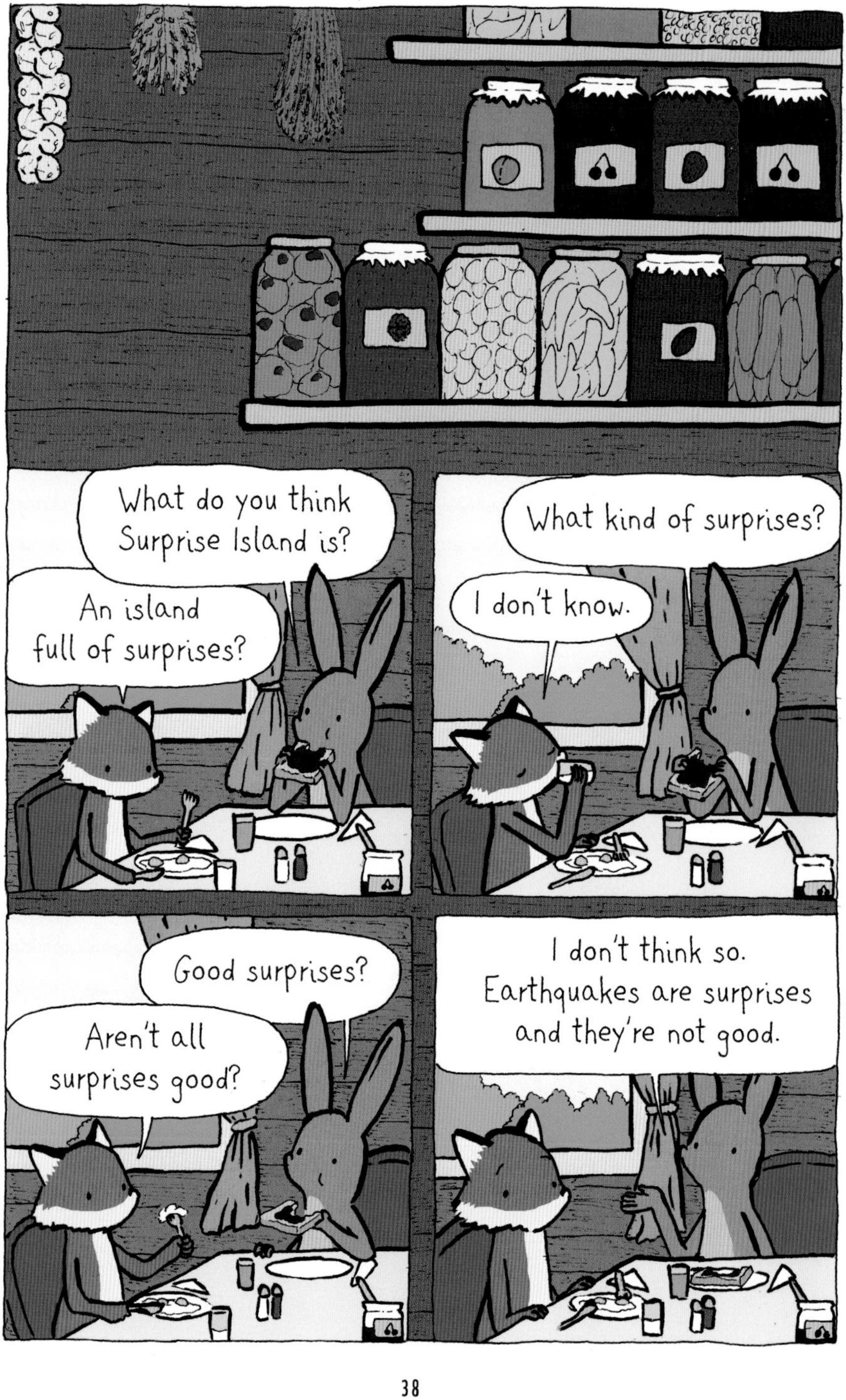
What do you think Surprise Island is?
An island full of surprises?
What kind of surprises?
I don't know.
Good surprises?
Aren't all surprises good?
I don't think so. Earthquakes are surprises and they're not good.

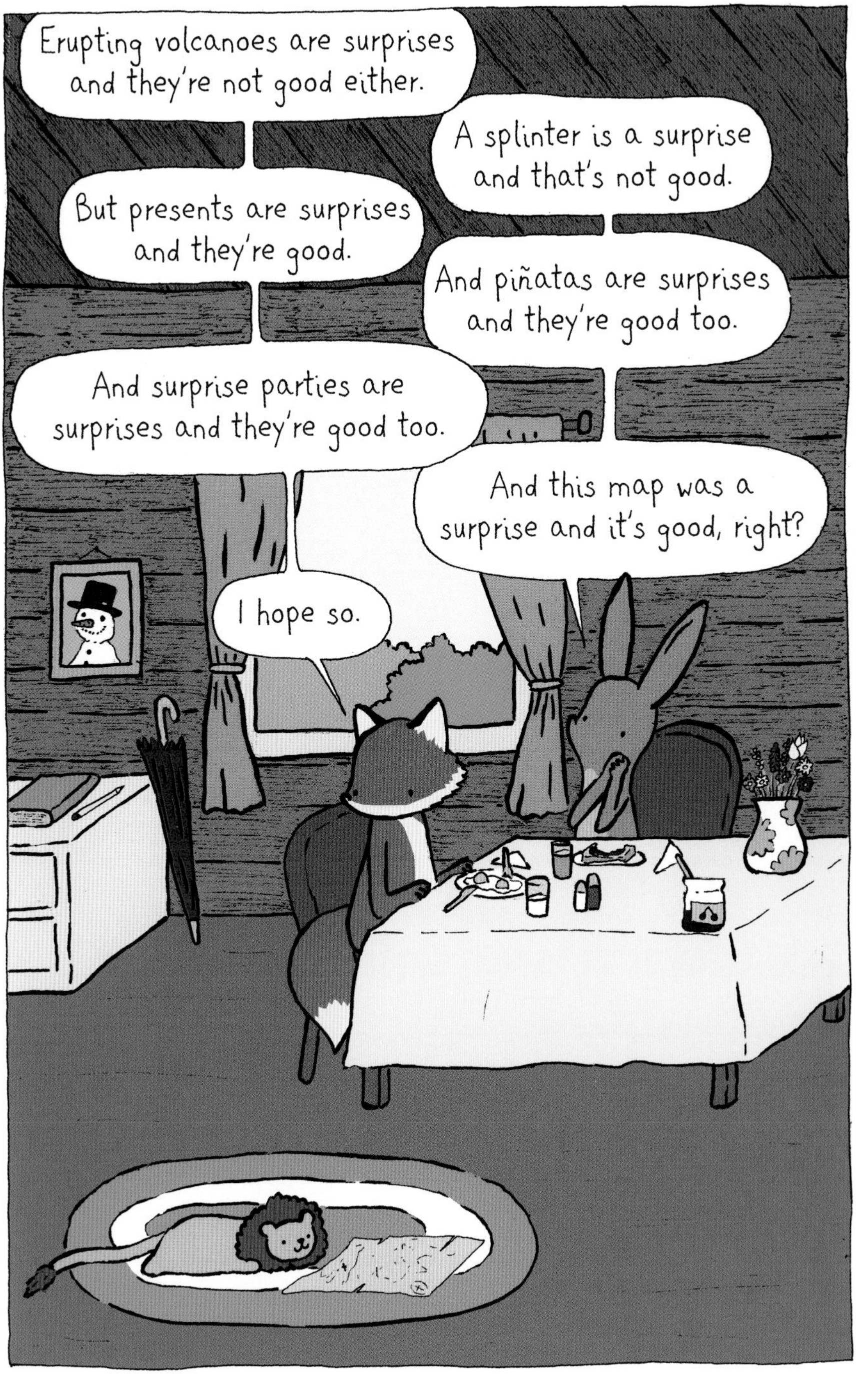
Erupting volcanoes are surprises and they're not good either.
A splinter is a surprise and that's not good.
But presents are surprises and they're good.
And piñatas are surprises and they're good too.
And surprise parties are surprises and they're good too.
And this map was a surprise and it's good, right?
I hope so.

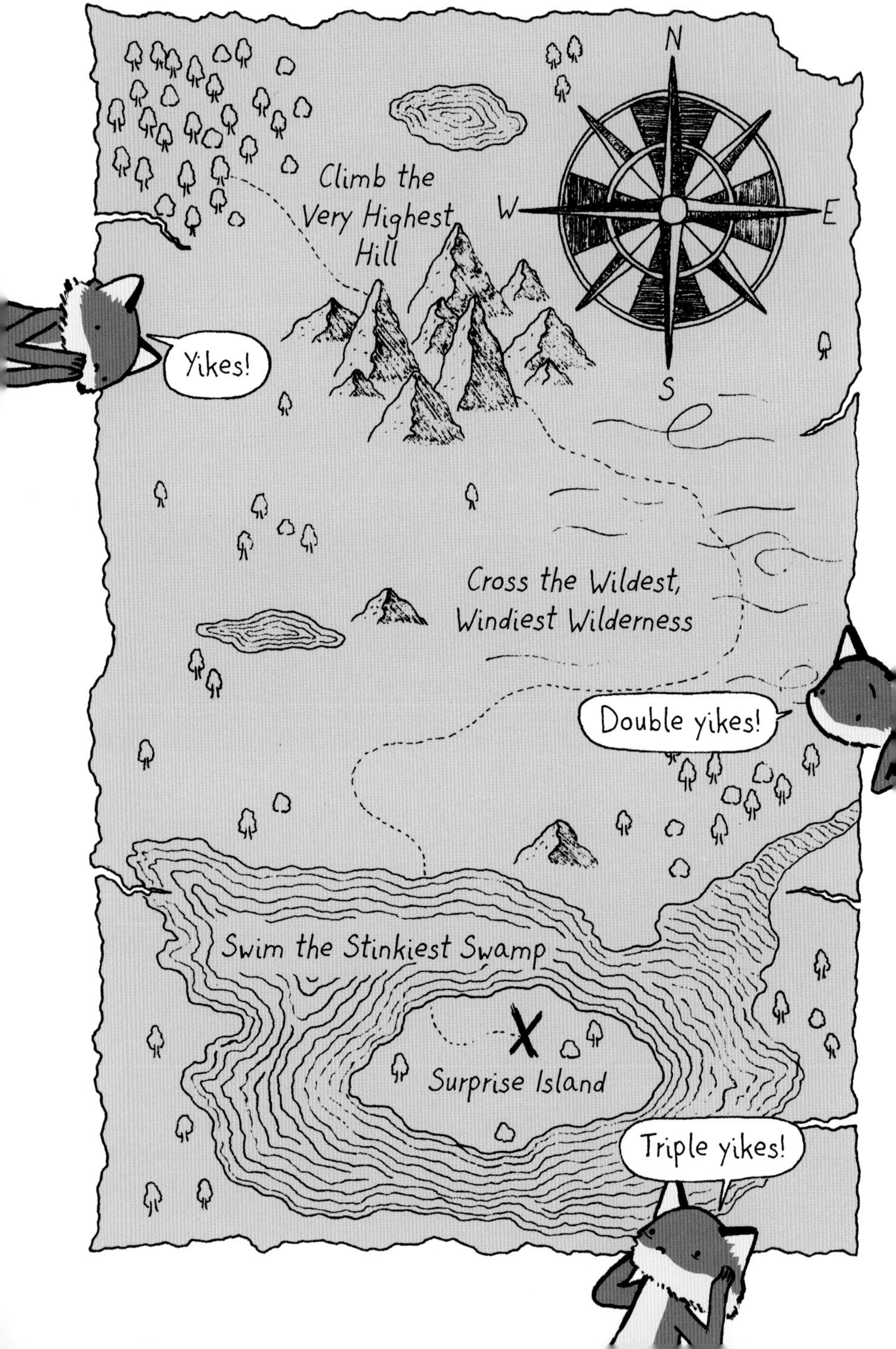
N
W
E
S
Climb the Very Highest Hill
Yikes!
Cross the Wildest, Windiest Wilderness
Double yikes!
Swim the Stinkiest Swamp
Surprise Island
Triple yikes!

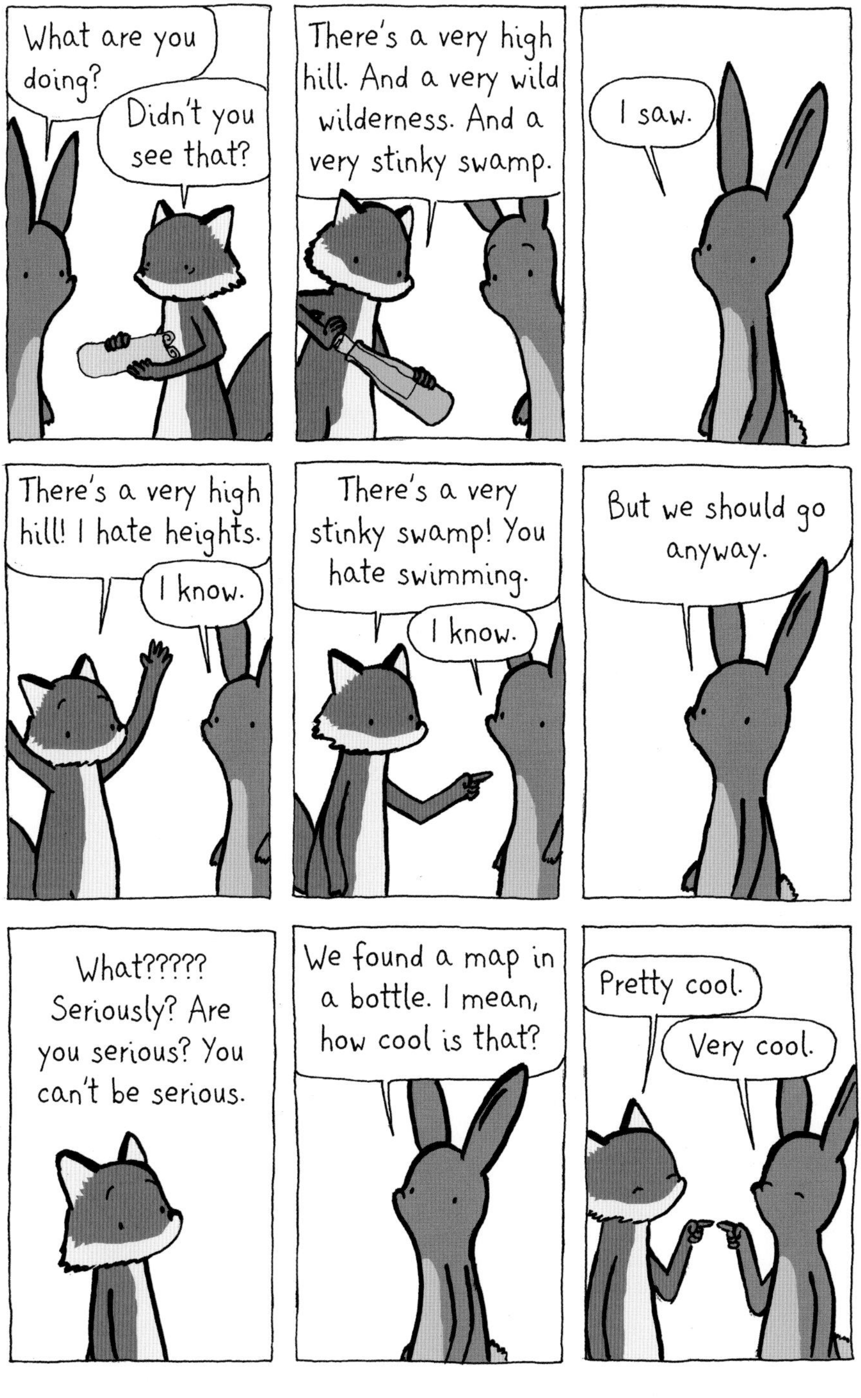
What are you doing?
Didn't you see that?
There's a very high hill. And a very wild wilderness. And a very stinky swamp.
I saw.
There's a very high hill! I hate heights.
I know.
There's a very stinky swamp! You hate swimming.
I know.
But we should go anyway.
What????? Seriously? Are you serious? You can't be serious.
We found a map in a bottle. I mean, how cool is that?
Pretty cool.
Very cool.

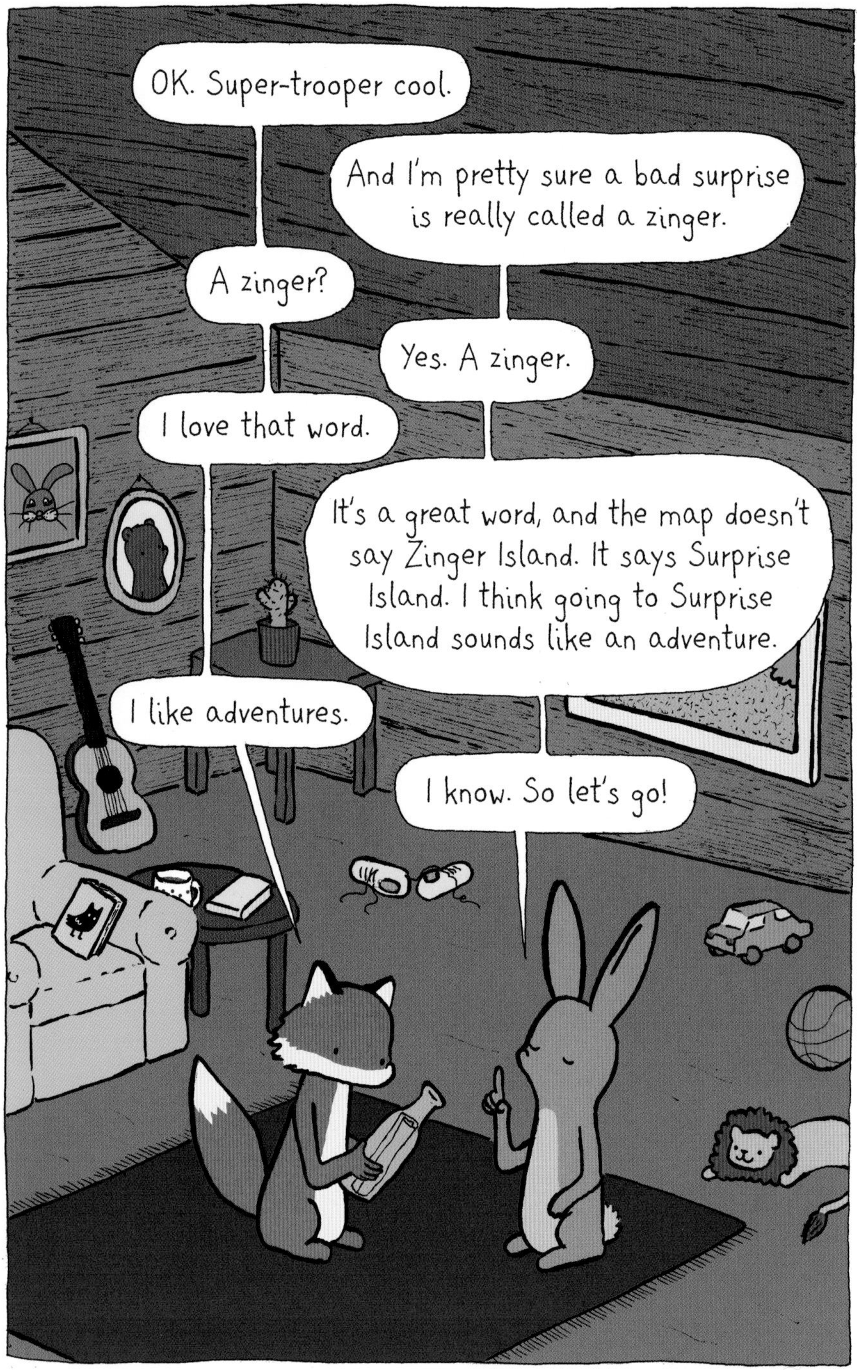
OK. Super-trooper cool.
And I'm pretty sure a bad surprise is really called a zinger.
A zinger?
Yes. A zinger.
I love that word.
It's a great word, and the map doesn't say Zinger Island. It says Surprise Island. I think going to Surprise Island sounds like an adventure.
I like adventures.
I know. So let's go!

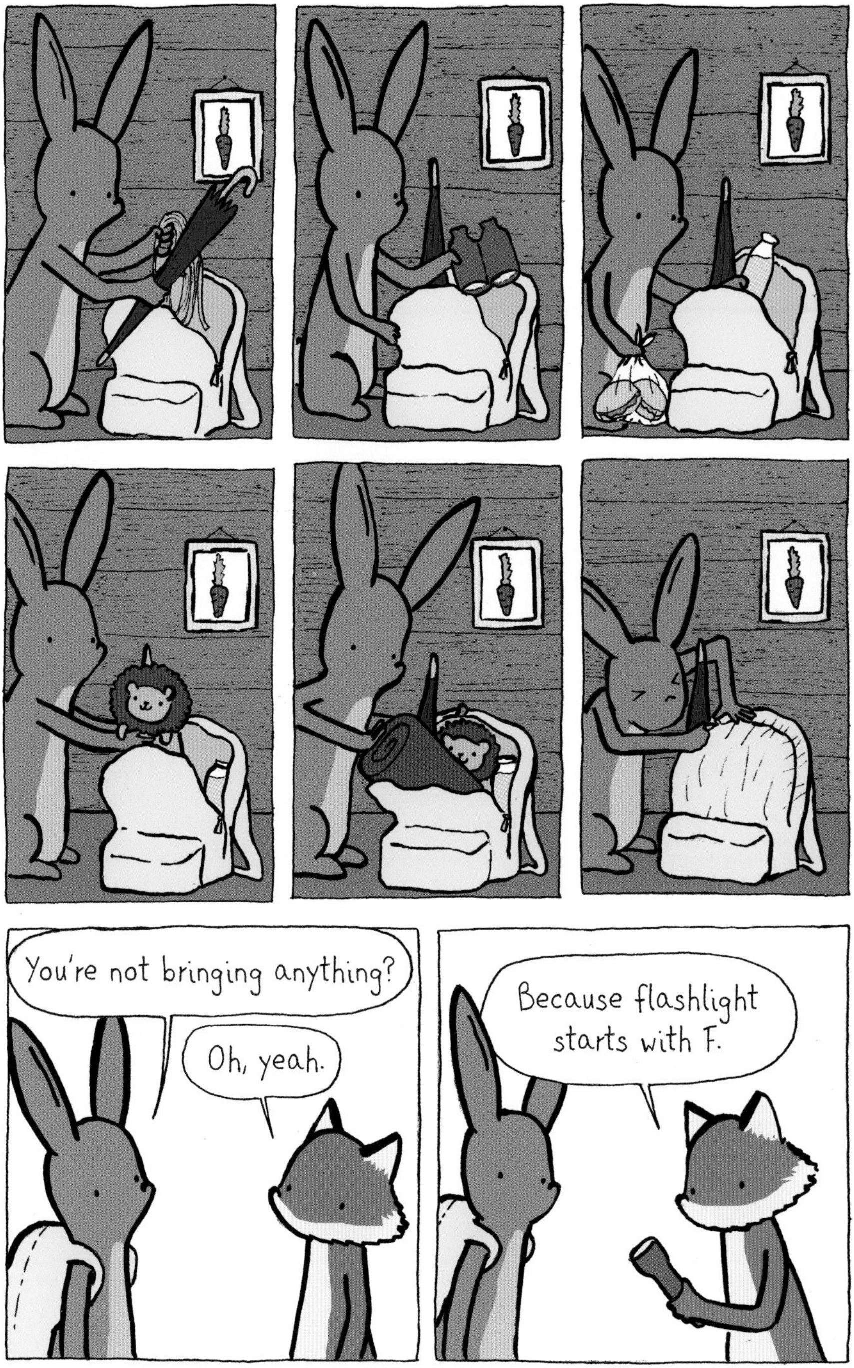
You're not bringing anything?
Oh, yeah.
Because flashlight starts with F.

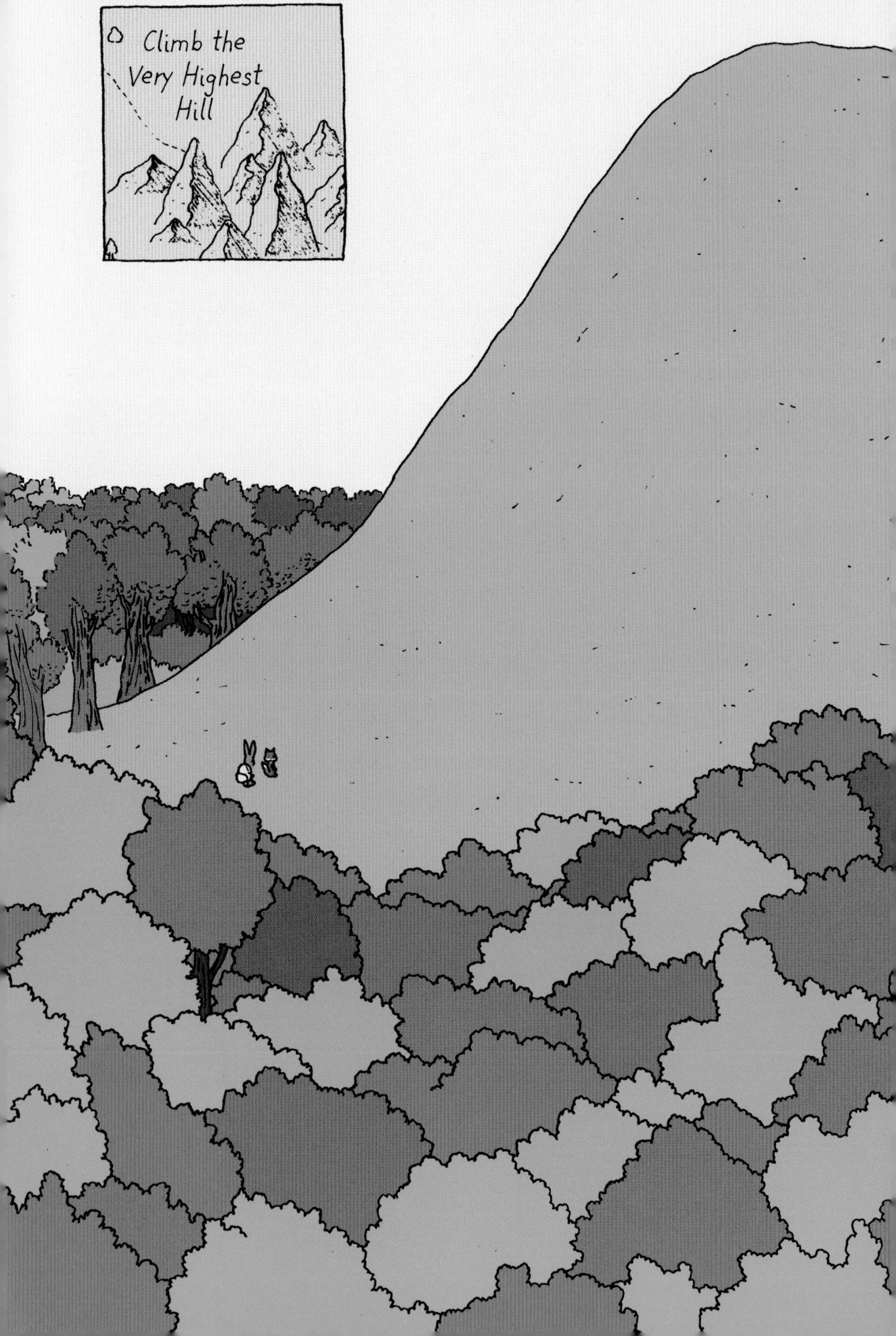
Climb the Very Highest Hill

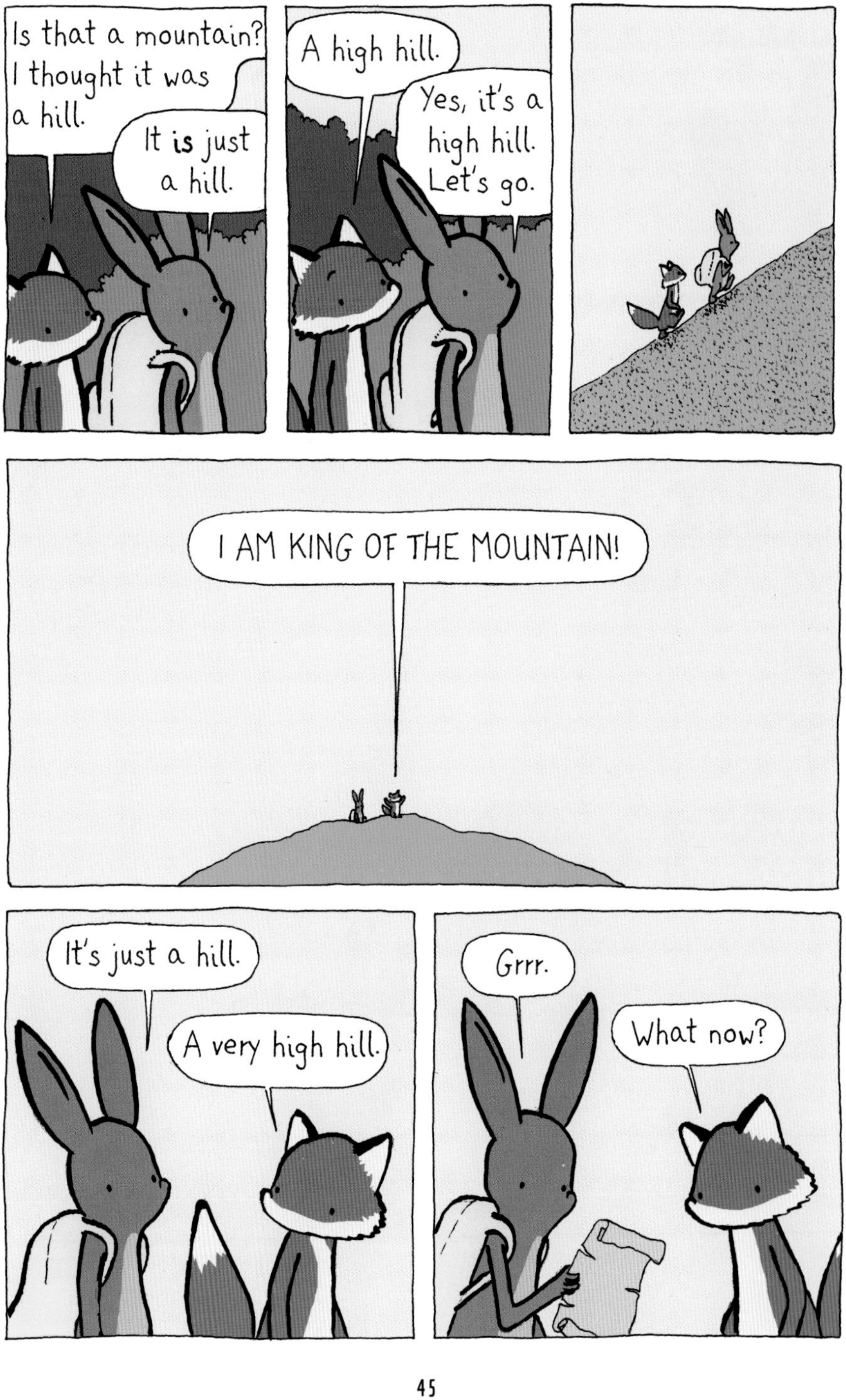
Is that a mountain? I thought it was a hill.
It **is** just a hill.
A high hill.
Yes, it's a high hill. Let's go.
I AM KING OF THE MOUNTAIN!
It's just a hill.
A very high hill.
Grrr.
What now?

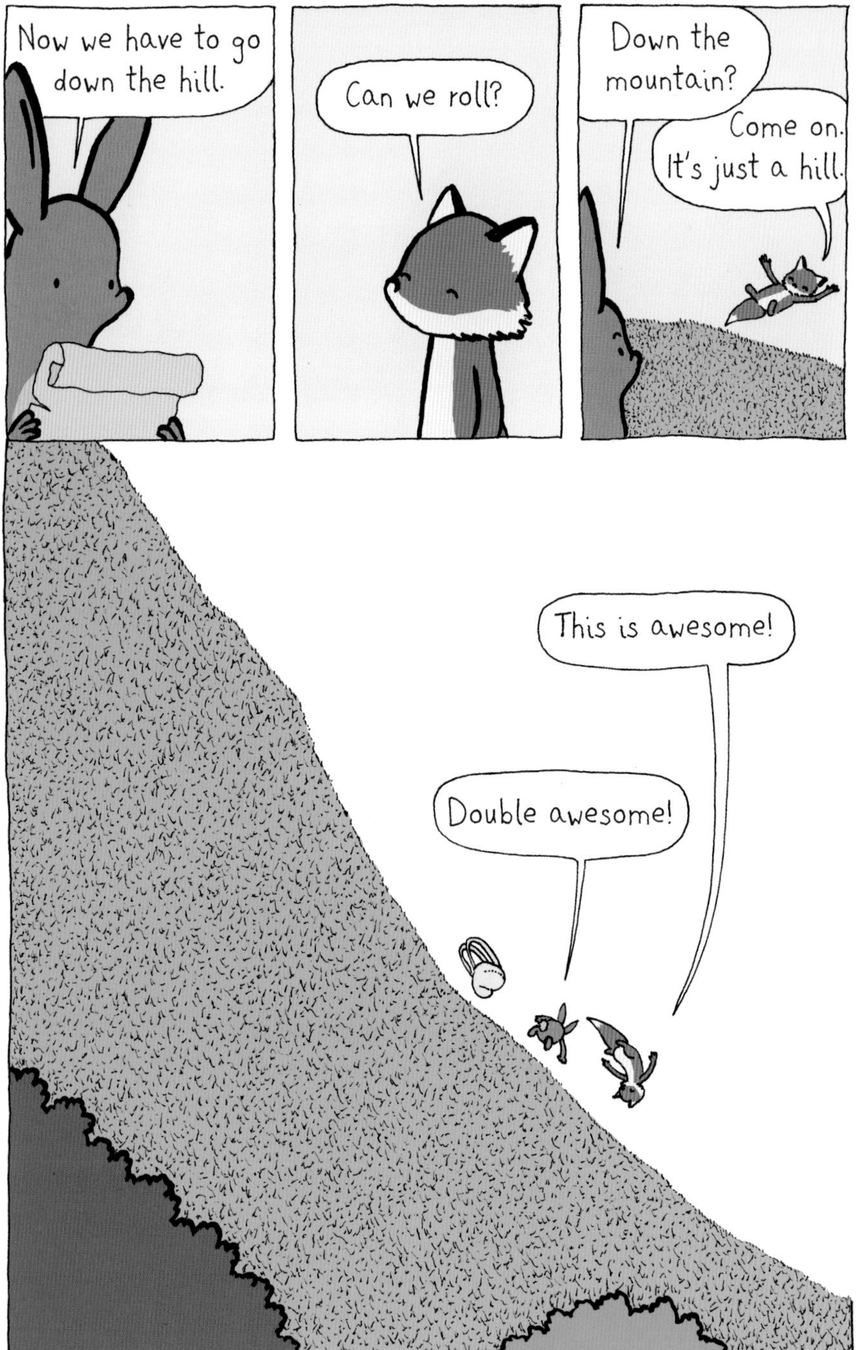
Now we have to go down the hill.
Can we roll?
Down the mountain?
Come on. It's just a hill.
This is awesome!
Double awesome!

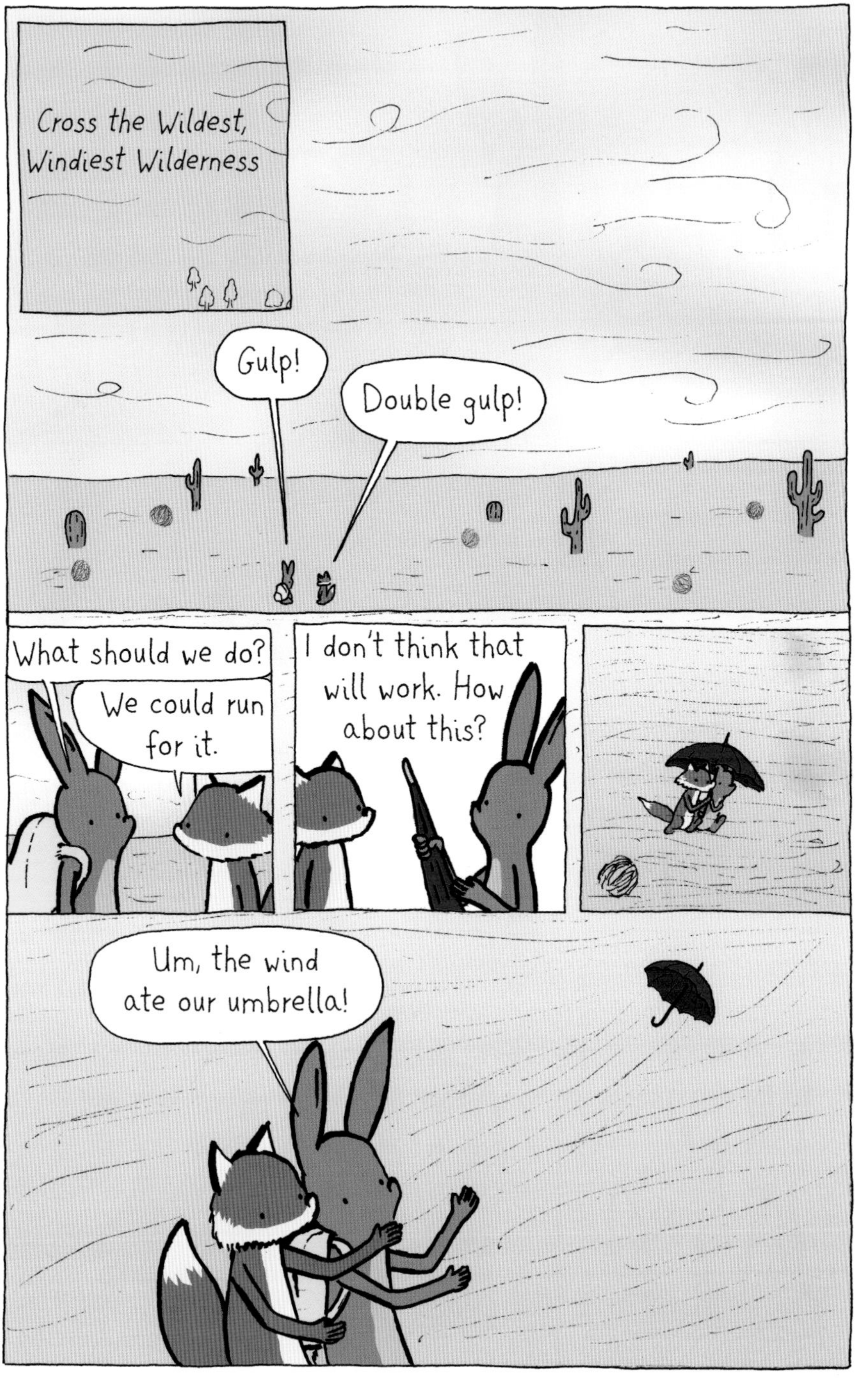

Cross the Wildest, Windiest Wilderness
Gulp!
Double gulp!
What should we do?
We could run for it.
I don't think that will work. How about this?
Um, the wind ate our umbrella!

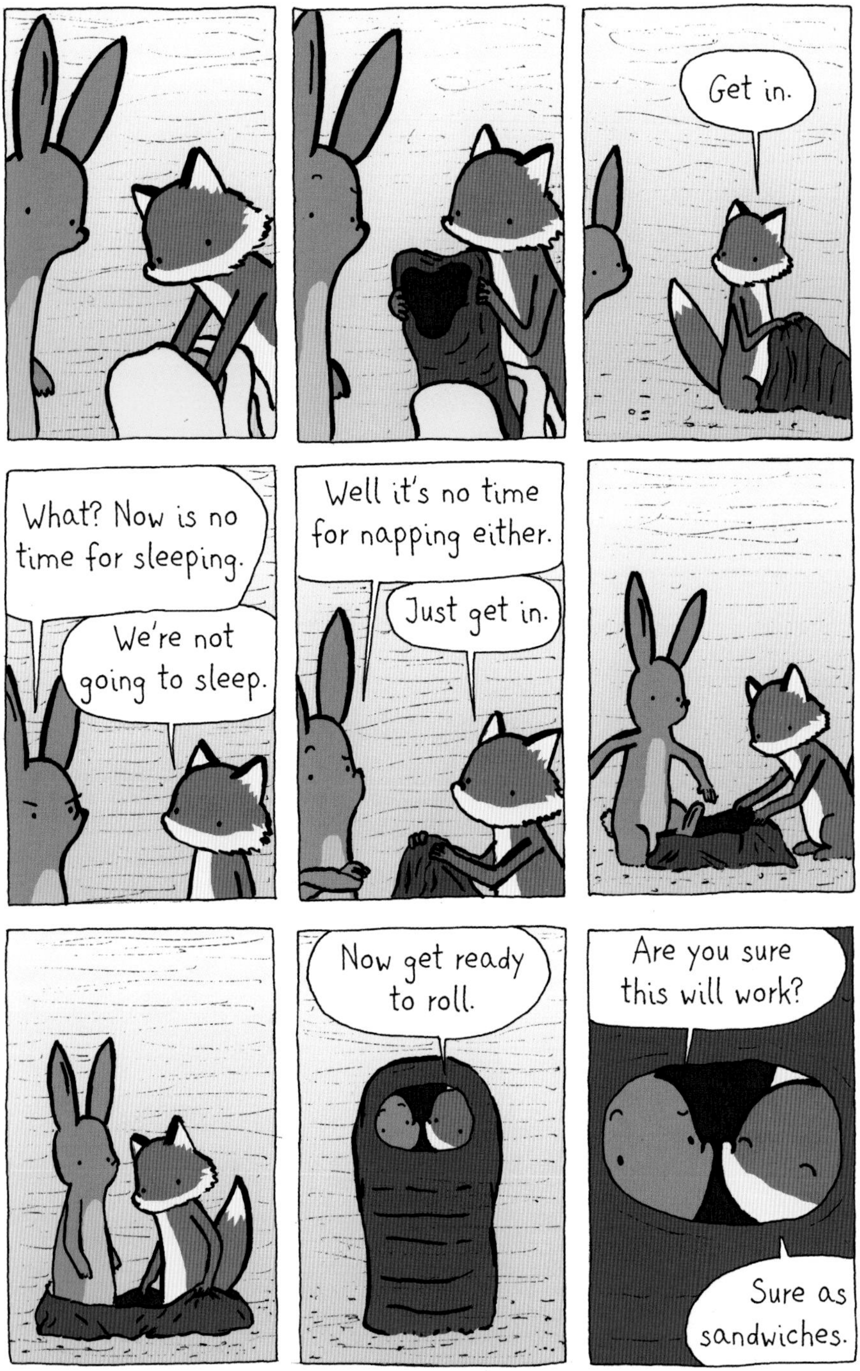
Get in.
What? Now is no time for sleeping.
We're not going to sleep.
Well it's no time for napping either.
Just get in.
Now get ready to roll.
Are you sure this will work?
Sure as sandwiches.

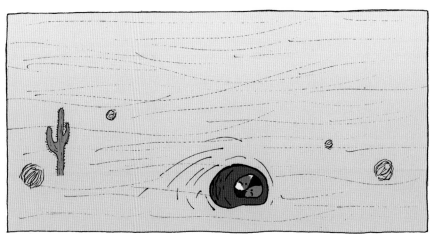

It worked!

Of course it did. And I could really use a sandwich.

Hooray! We're almost there!

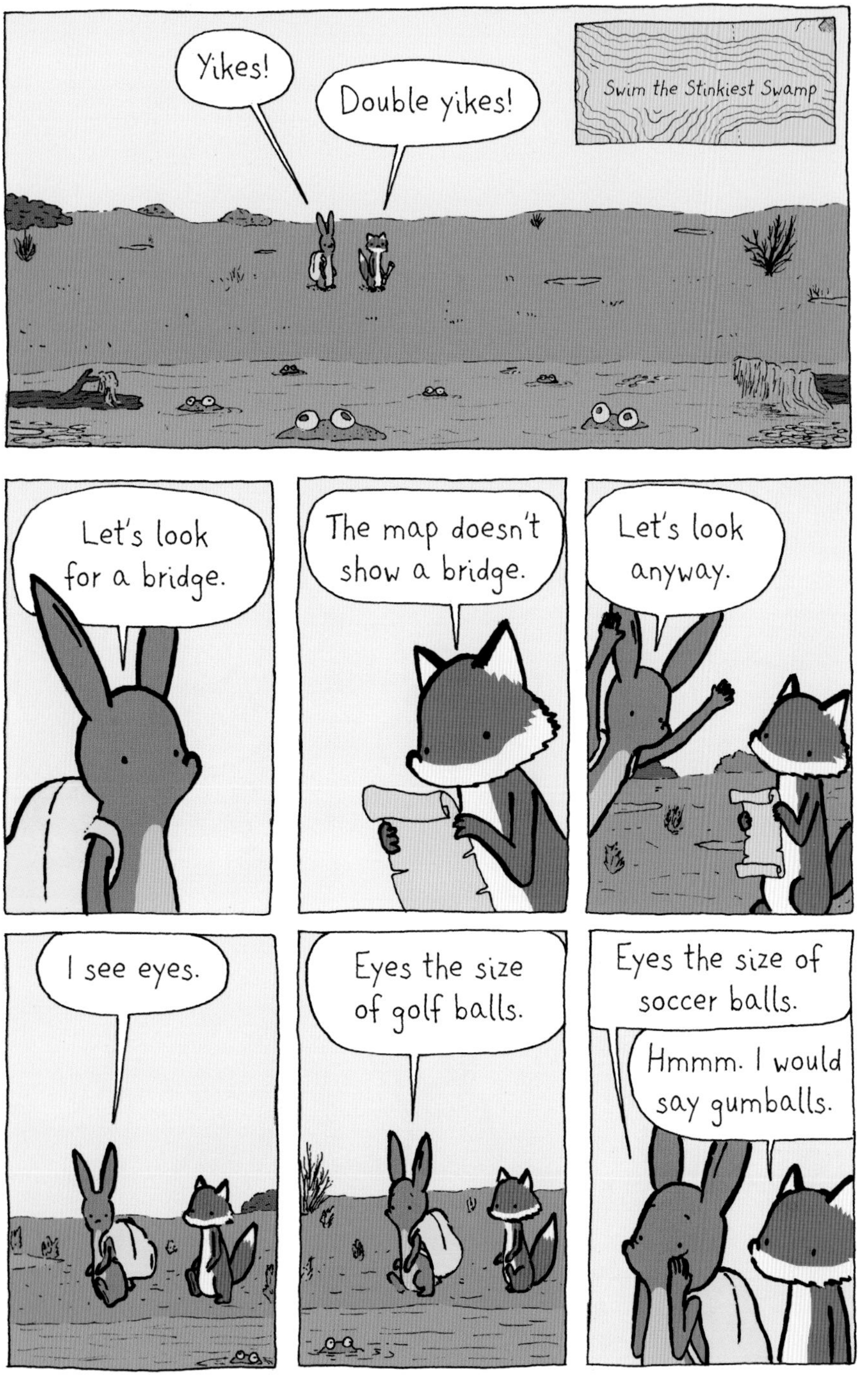
Yikes!
Double yikes!
Swim the Stinkiest Swamp
Let's look for a bridge.
The map doesn't show a bridge.
Let's look anyway.
I see eyes.
Eyes the size of golf balls.
Eyes the size of soccer balls.
Hmmm. I would say gumballs.

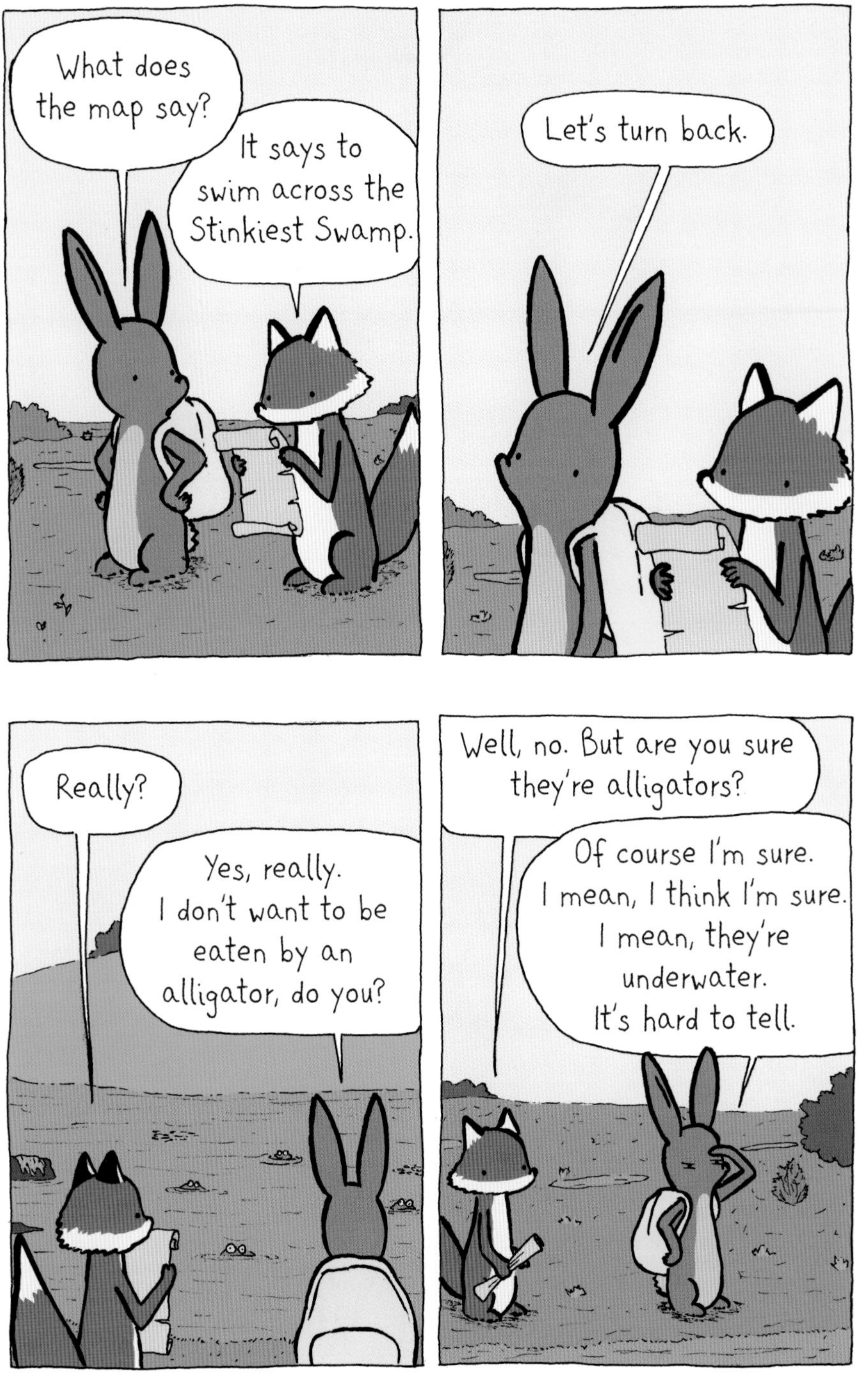
What does the map say?
It says to swim across the Stinkiest Swamp.
Let's turn back.
Really?
Yes, really. I don't want to be eaten by an alligator, do you?
Well, no. But are you sure they're alligators?
Of course I'm sure. I mean, I think I'm sure. I mean, they're underwater. It's hard to tell.

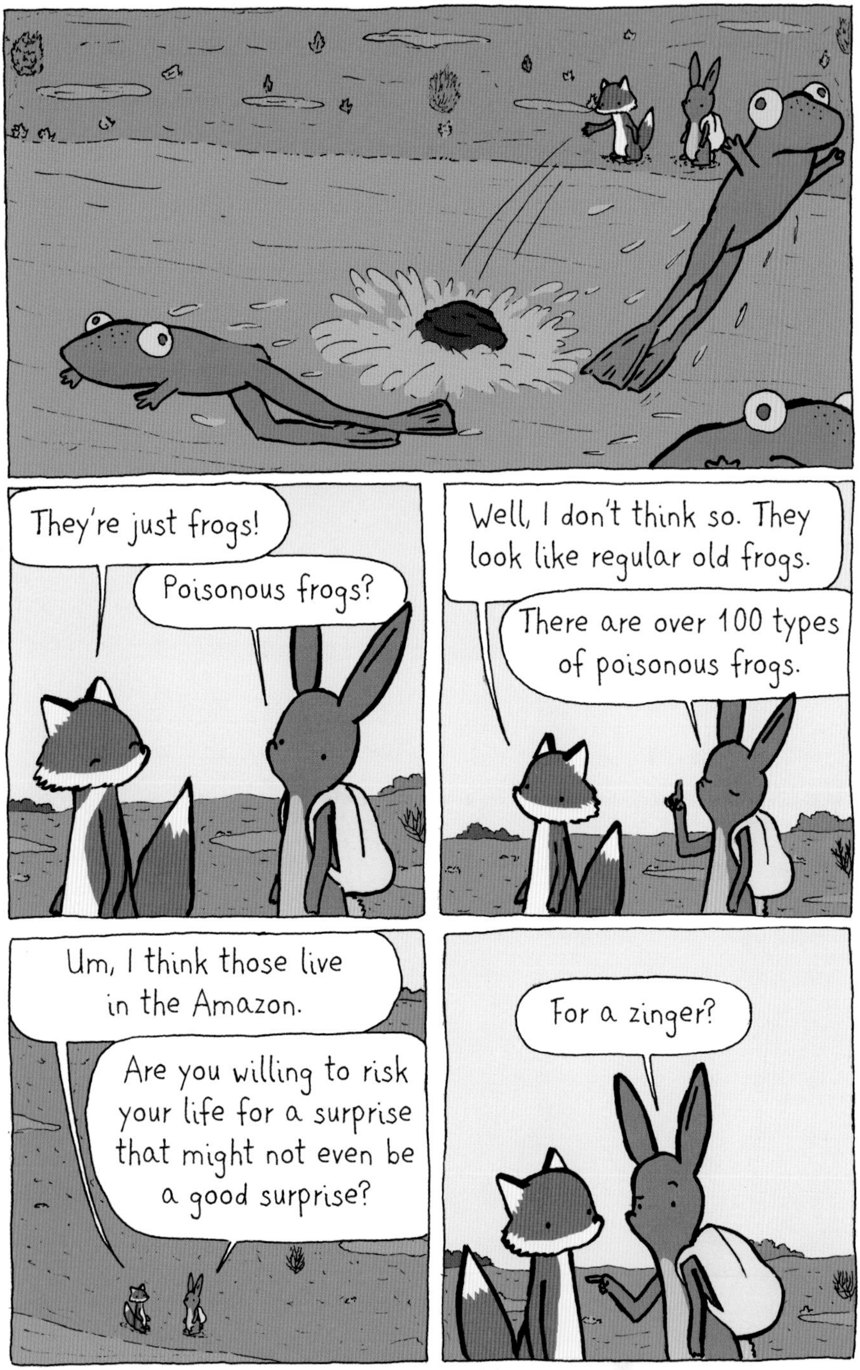
They're just frogs!
Poisonous frogs?
Well, I don't think so. They look like regular old frogs.
There are over 100 types of poisonous frogs.
Um, I think those live in the Amazon.
Are you willing to risk your life for a surprise that might not even be a good surprise?
For a zinger?

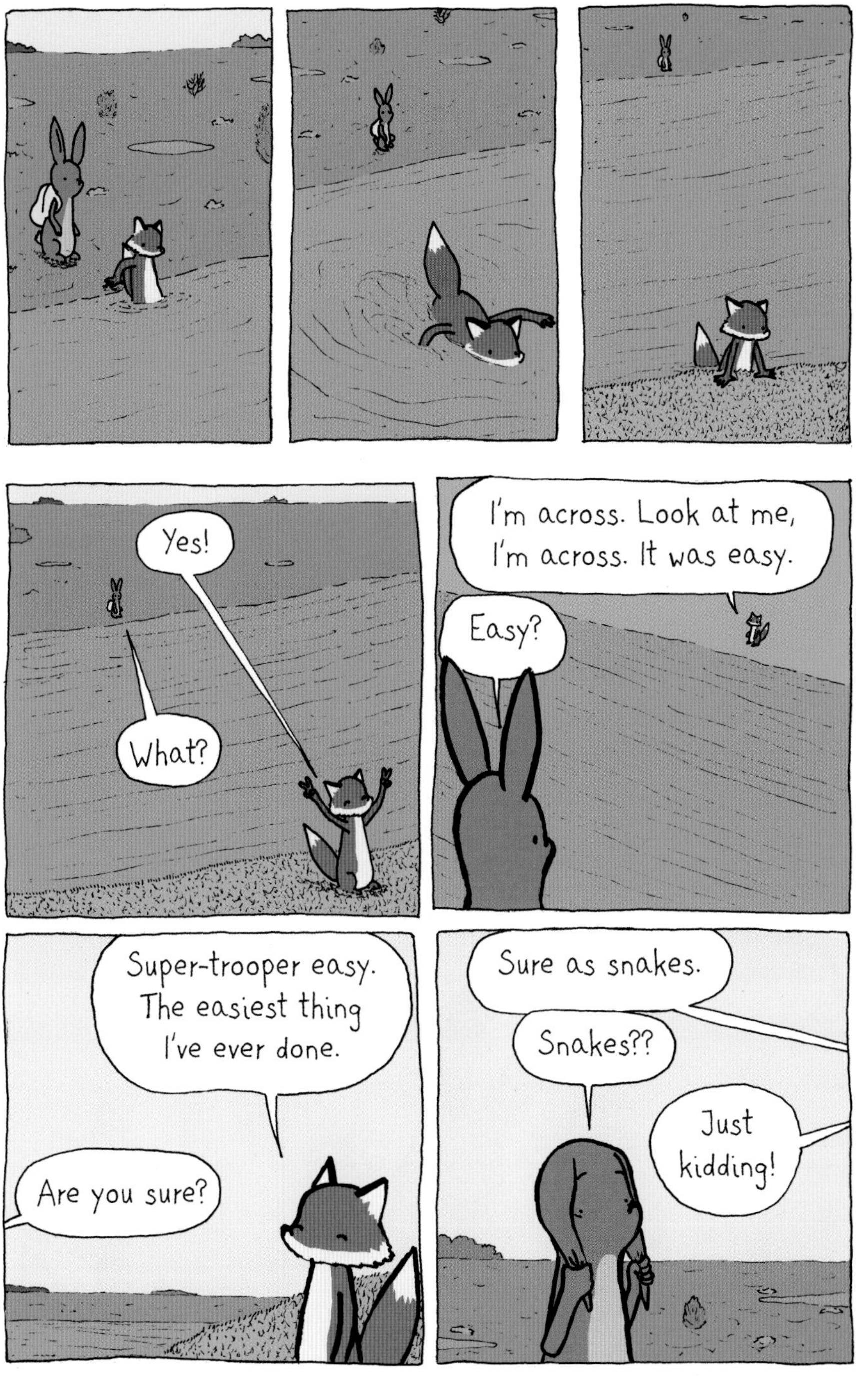
Yes!
What?
I'm across. Look at me, I'm across. It was easy.
Easy?
Super-trooper easy. The easiest thing I've ever done.
Are you sure?
Sure as snakes.
Snakes??
Just kidding!

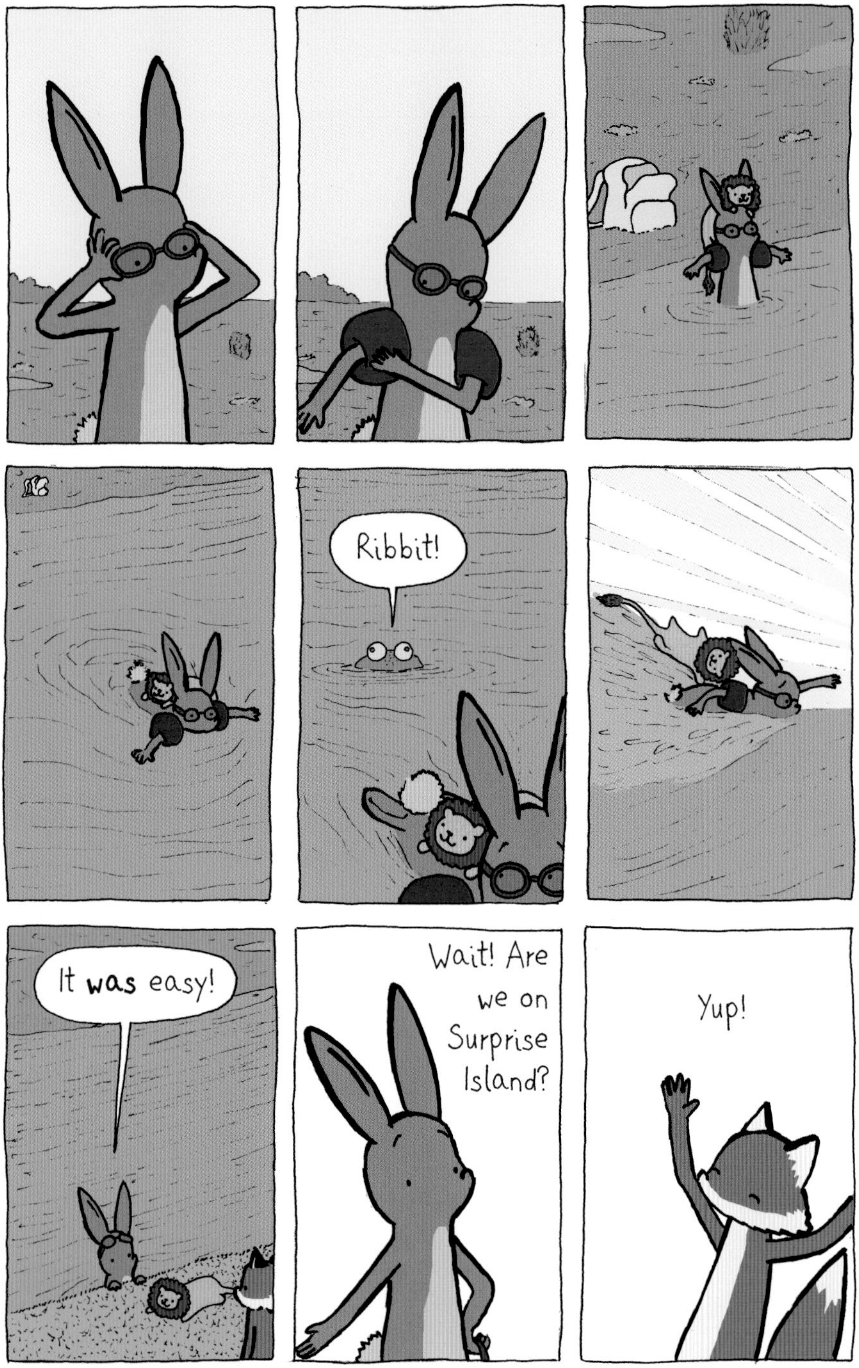
Ribbit!
It was easy!
Wait! Are we on Surprise Island?
Yup!

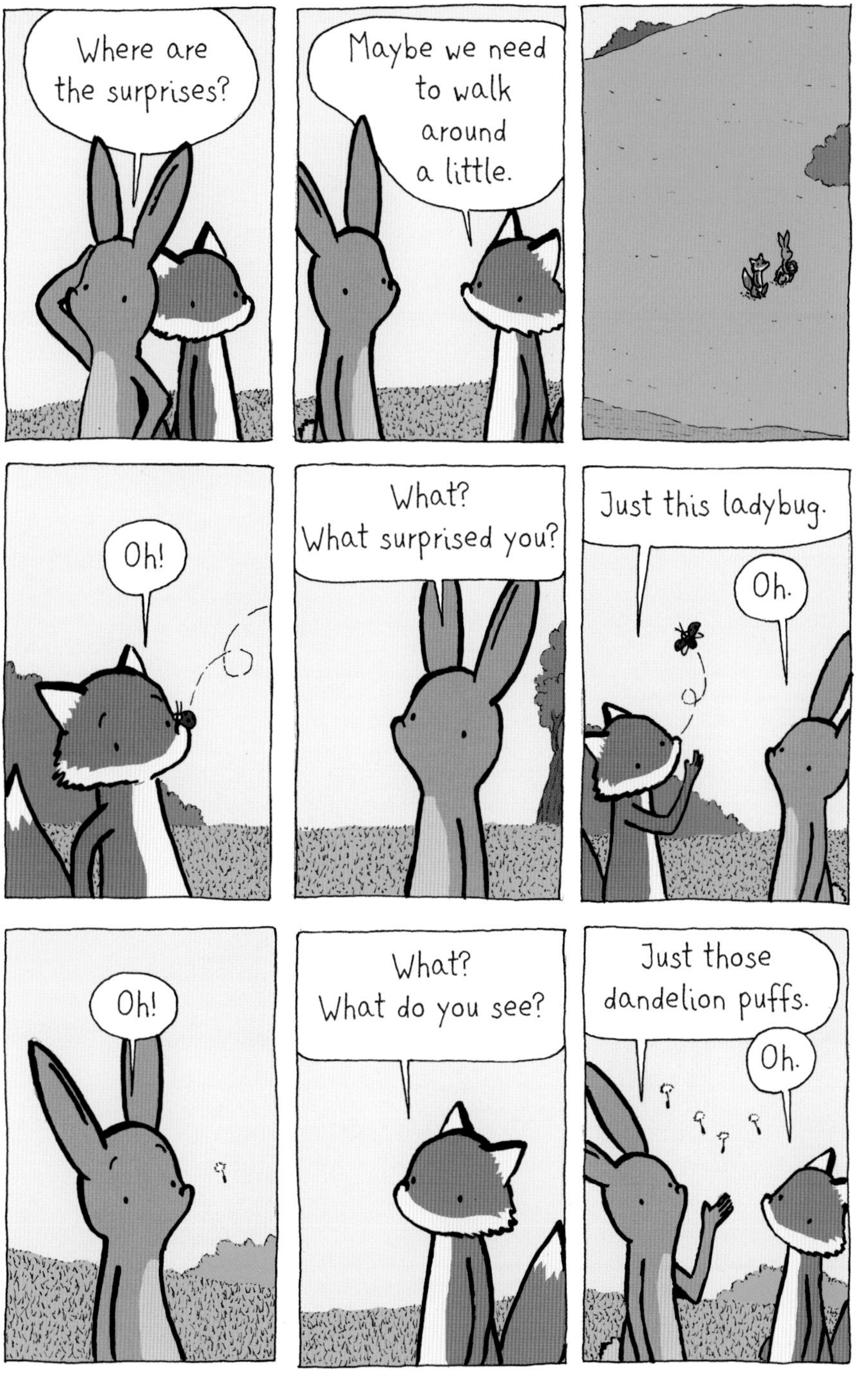
Where are the surprises?
Maybe we need to walk around a little.
Oh!
What? What surprised you?
Just this ladybug.
Oh.
Oh!
What? What do you see?
Just those dandelion puffs.
Oh.

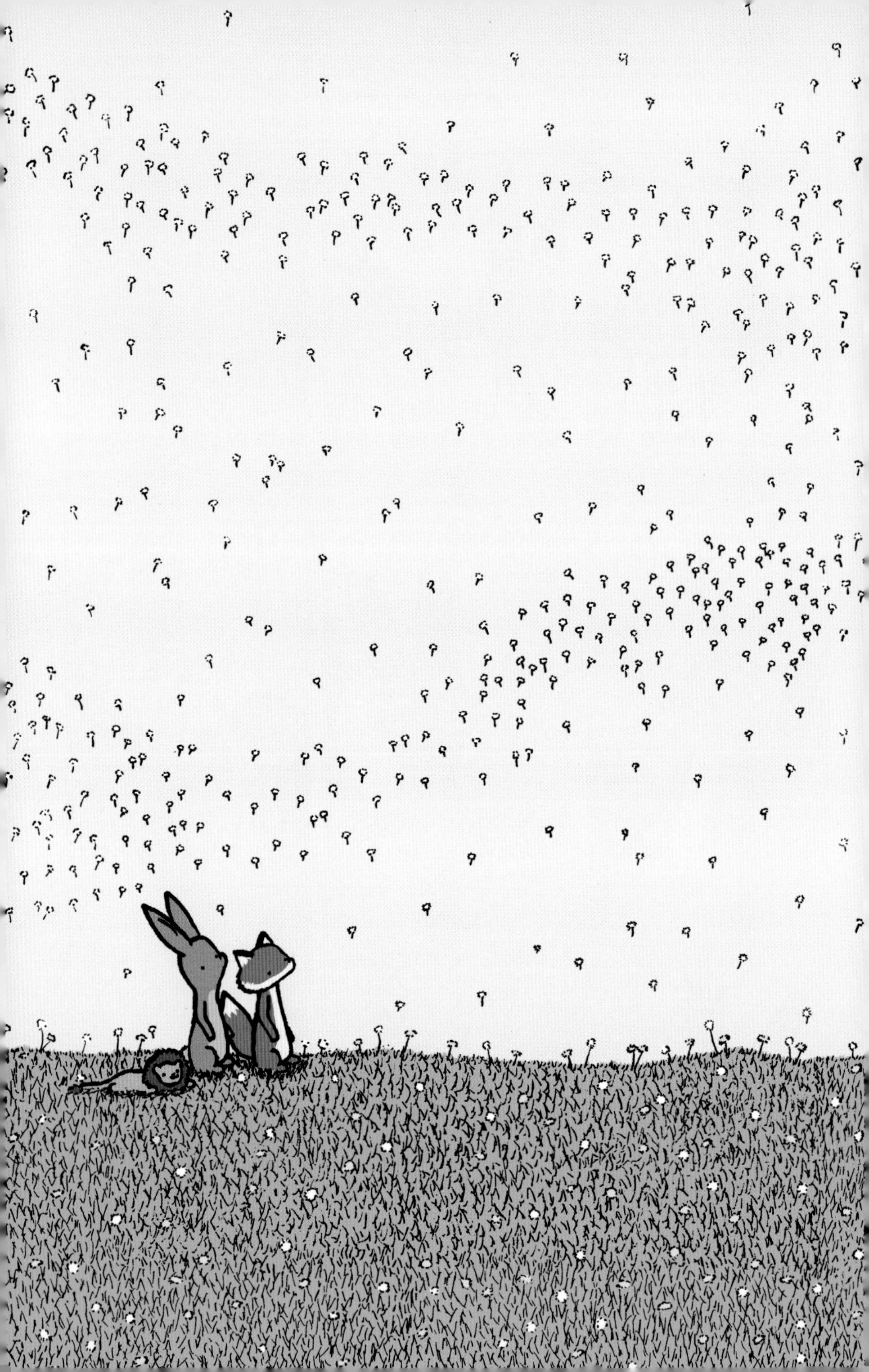

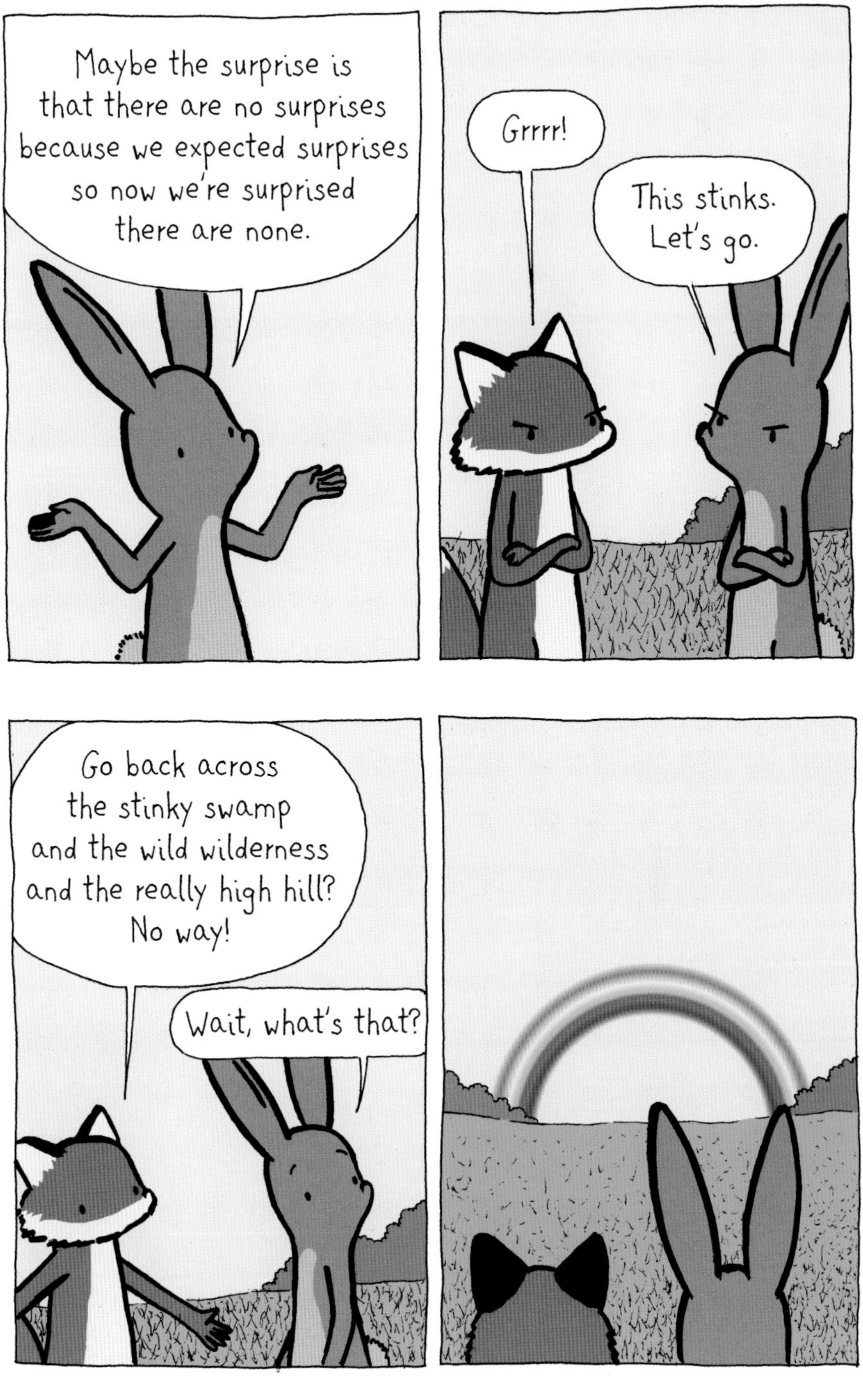
Maybe the surprise is that there are no surprises because we expected surprises so now we're surprised there are none.
Grrrr!
This stinks. Let's go.
Go back across the stinky swamp and the wild wilderness and the really high hill? No way!
Wait, what's that?

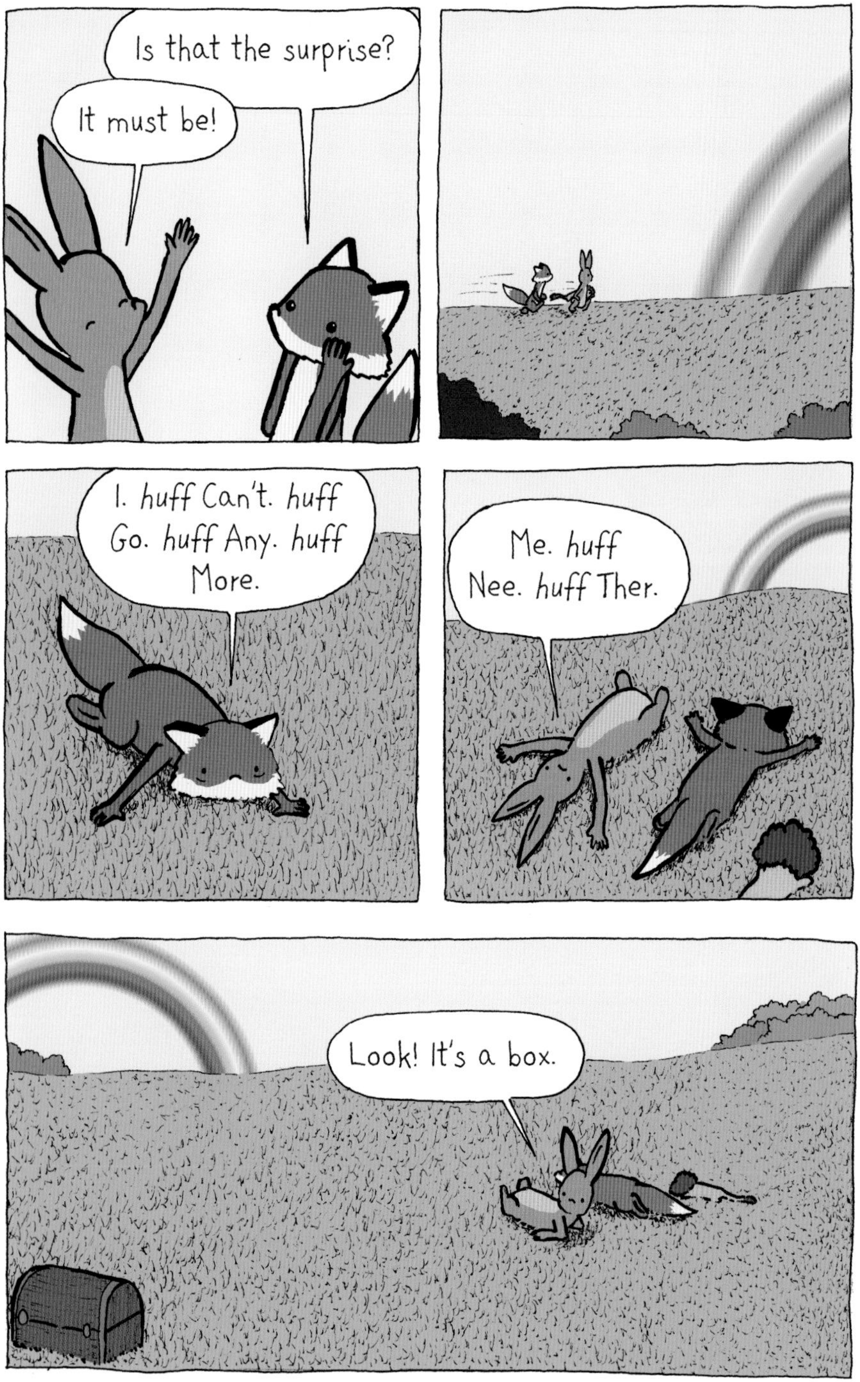
Is that the surprise?
It must be!
I. huff Can't. huff Go. huff Any. huff More.
Me. huff Nee. huff Ther.
Look! It's a box.

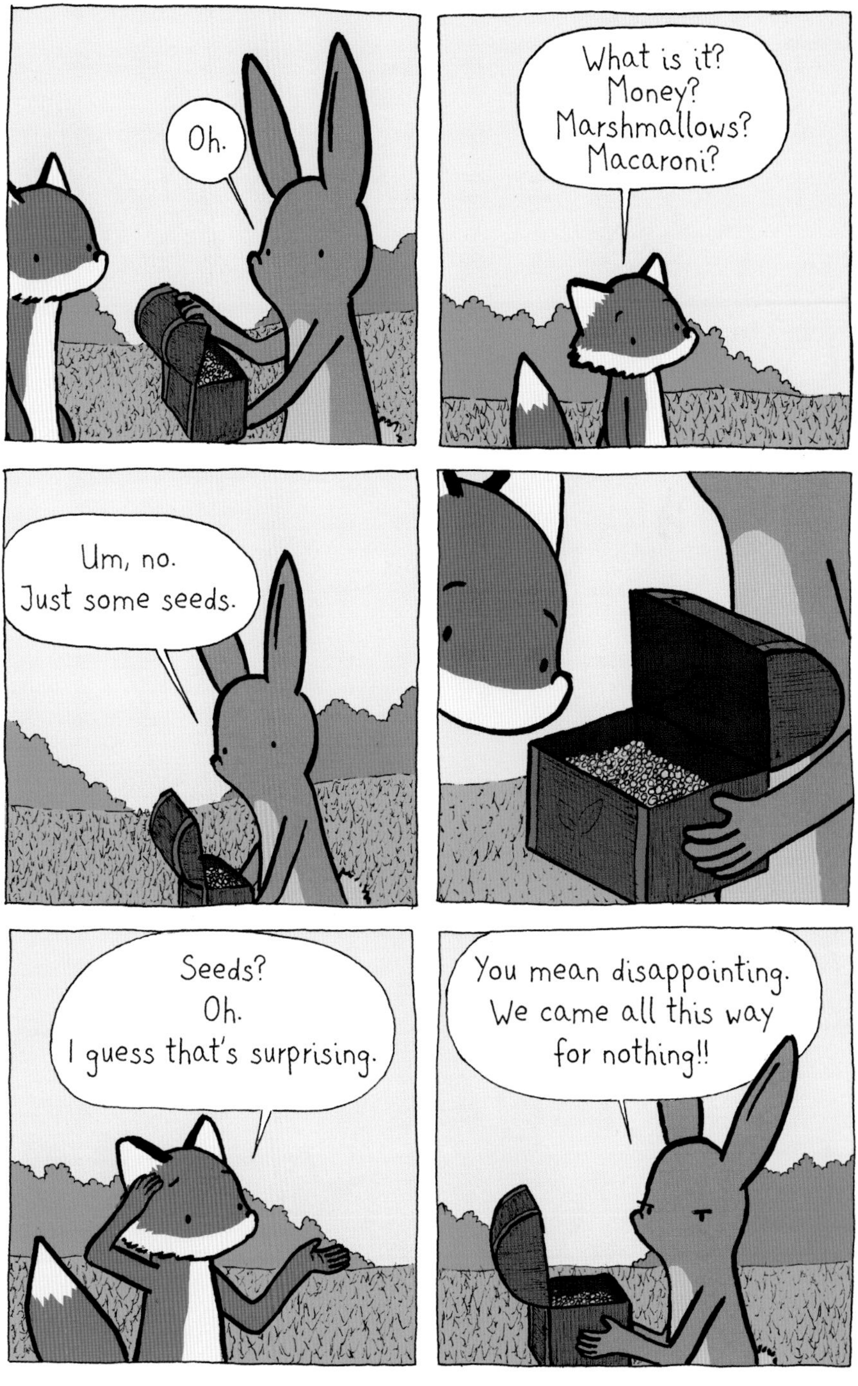
Oh.
What is it? Money? Marshmallows? Macaroni?
Um, no. Just some seeds.
Seeds? Oh. I guess that's surprising.
You mean disappointing. We came all this way for nothing!!

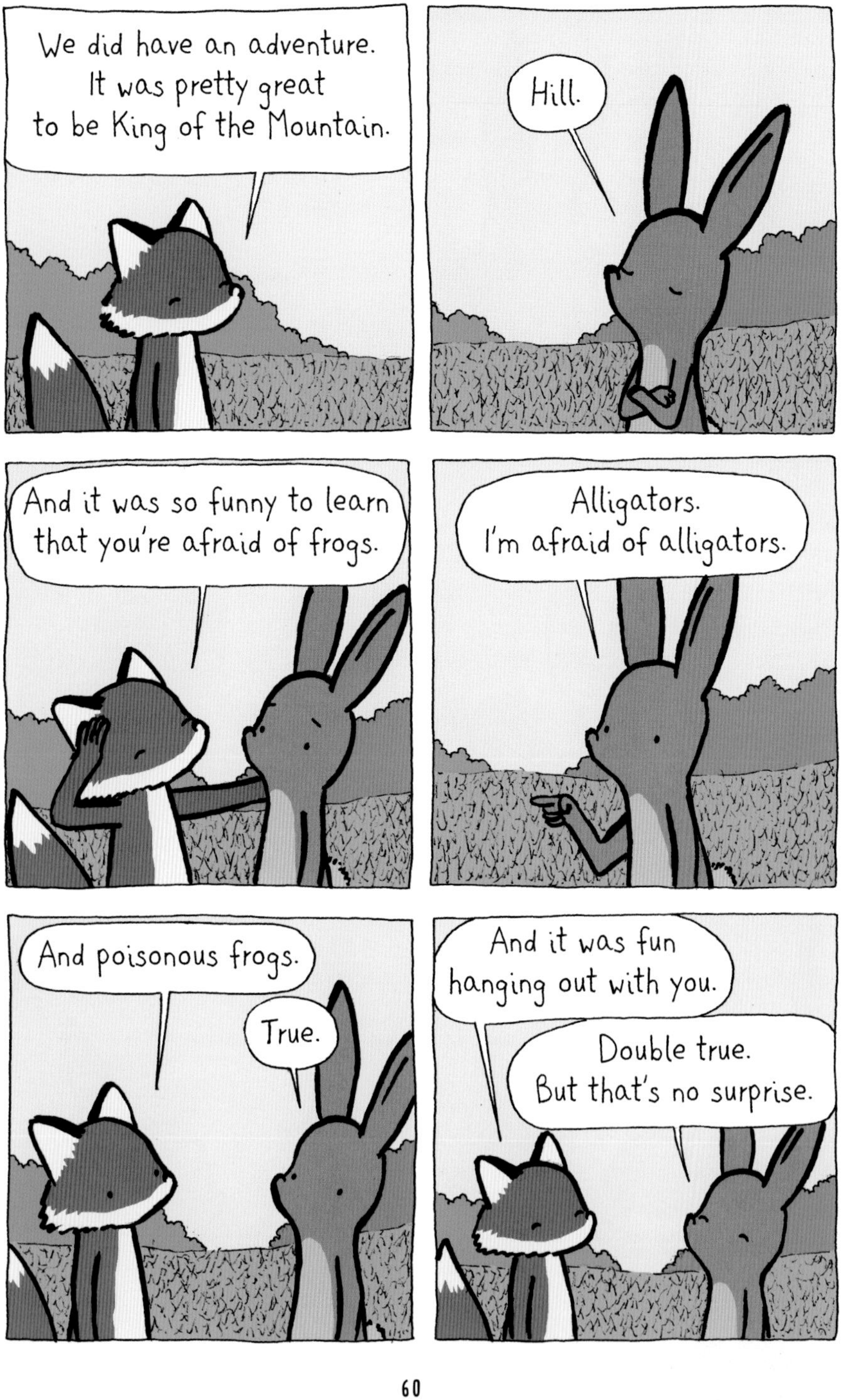
We did have an adventure. It was pretty great to be King of the Mountain.
Hill.
And it was so funny to learn that you're afraid of frogs.
Alligators. I'm afraid of alligators.
And poisonous frogs.
True.
And it was fun hanging out with you.
Double true. But that's no surprise.

Maybe surprises don't have to be big like piñatas or parties or volcanoes.

Yeah. Maybe surprises can just be ladybugs and rainbows.

Yeah. Or a day with your best friend.

Double yeah!

What'd I miss?

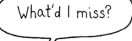

GARDENING, GROWING & GROANING

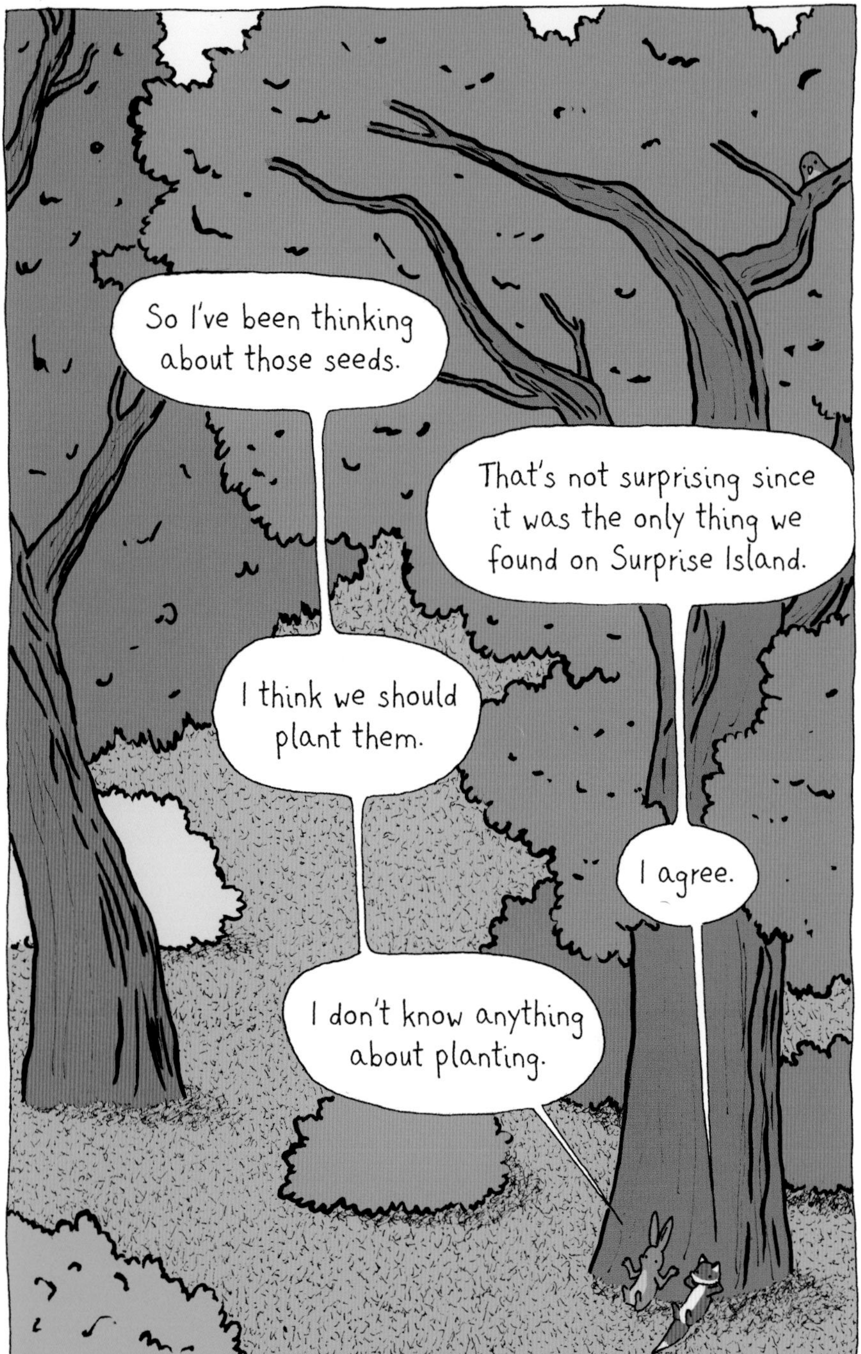
So I've been thinking about those seeds.
That's not surprising since it was the only thing we found on Surprise Island.
I think we should plant them.
I agree.
I don't know anything about planting.

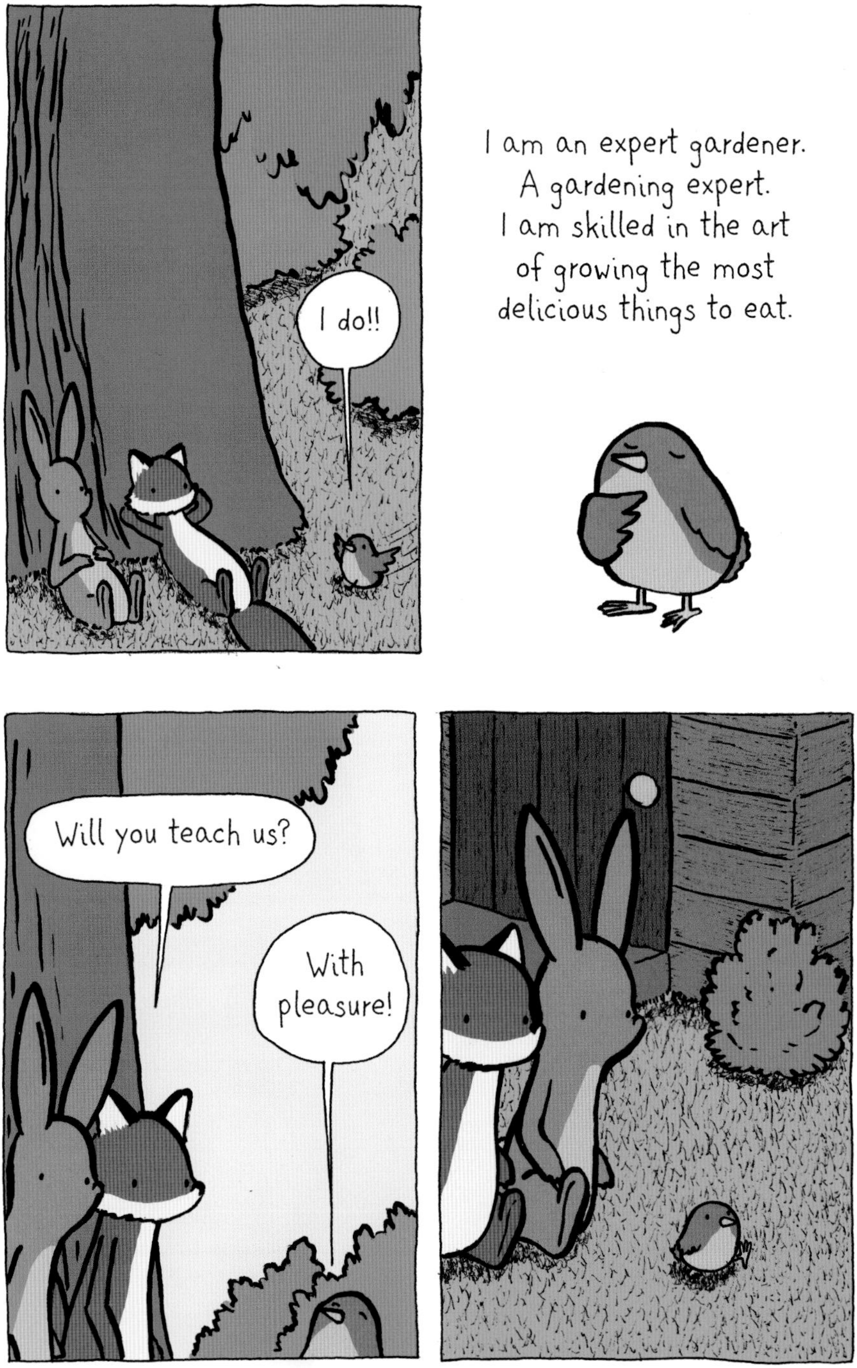
I do!!
I am an expert gardener. A gardening expert. I am skilled in the art of growing the most delicious things to eat.
Will you teach us?
With pleasure!

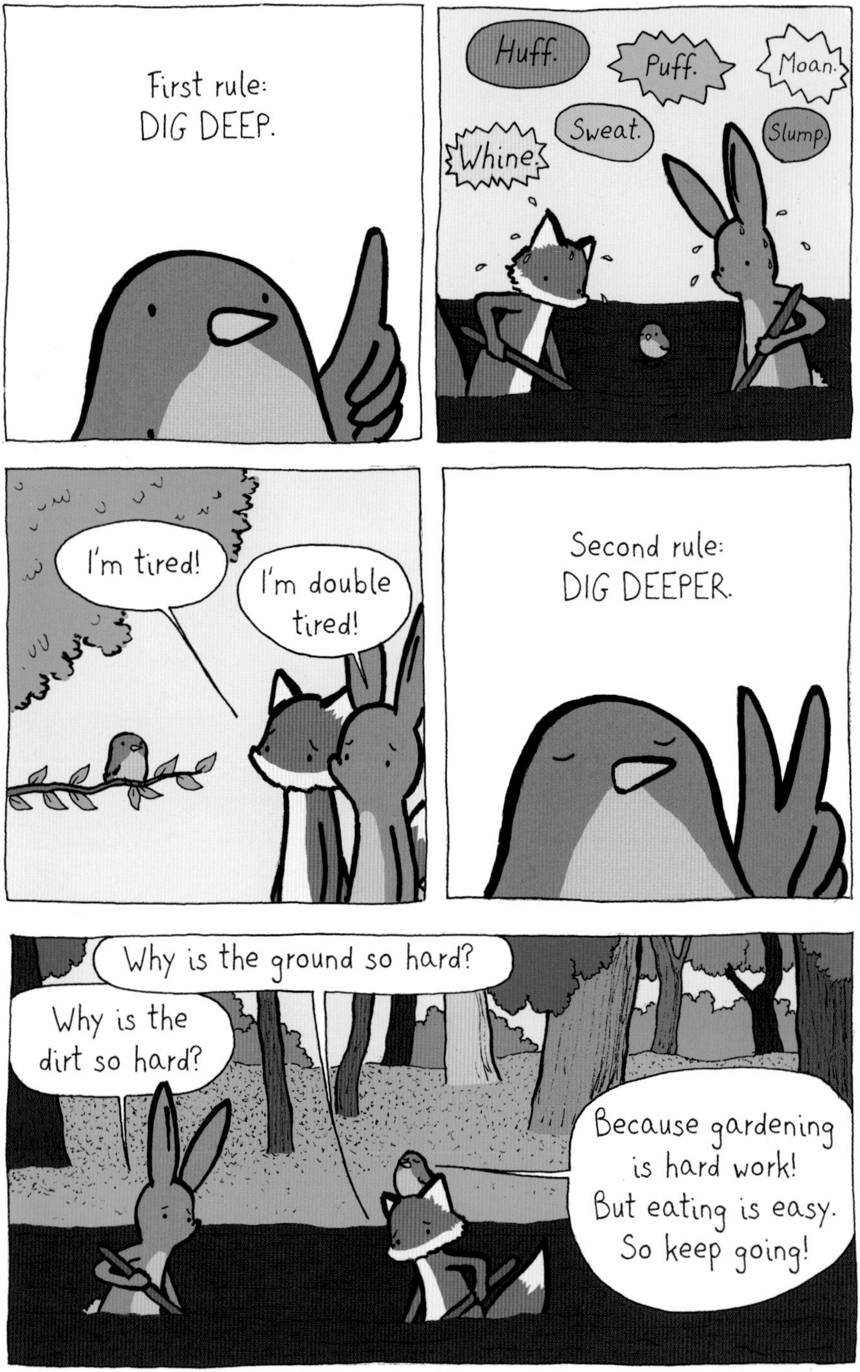
First rule:
DIG DEEP.
Huff.
Puff.
Moan.
Whine.
Sweat.
Slump.
I'm tired!
I'm double tired!
Second rule:
DIG DEEPER.
Why is the ground so hard?
Why is the dirt so hard?
Because gardening is hard work! But eating is easy. So keep going!

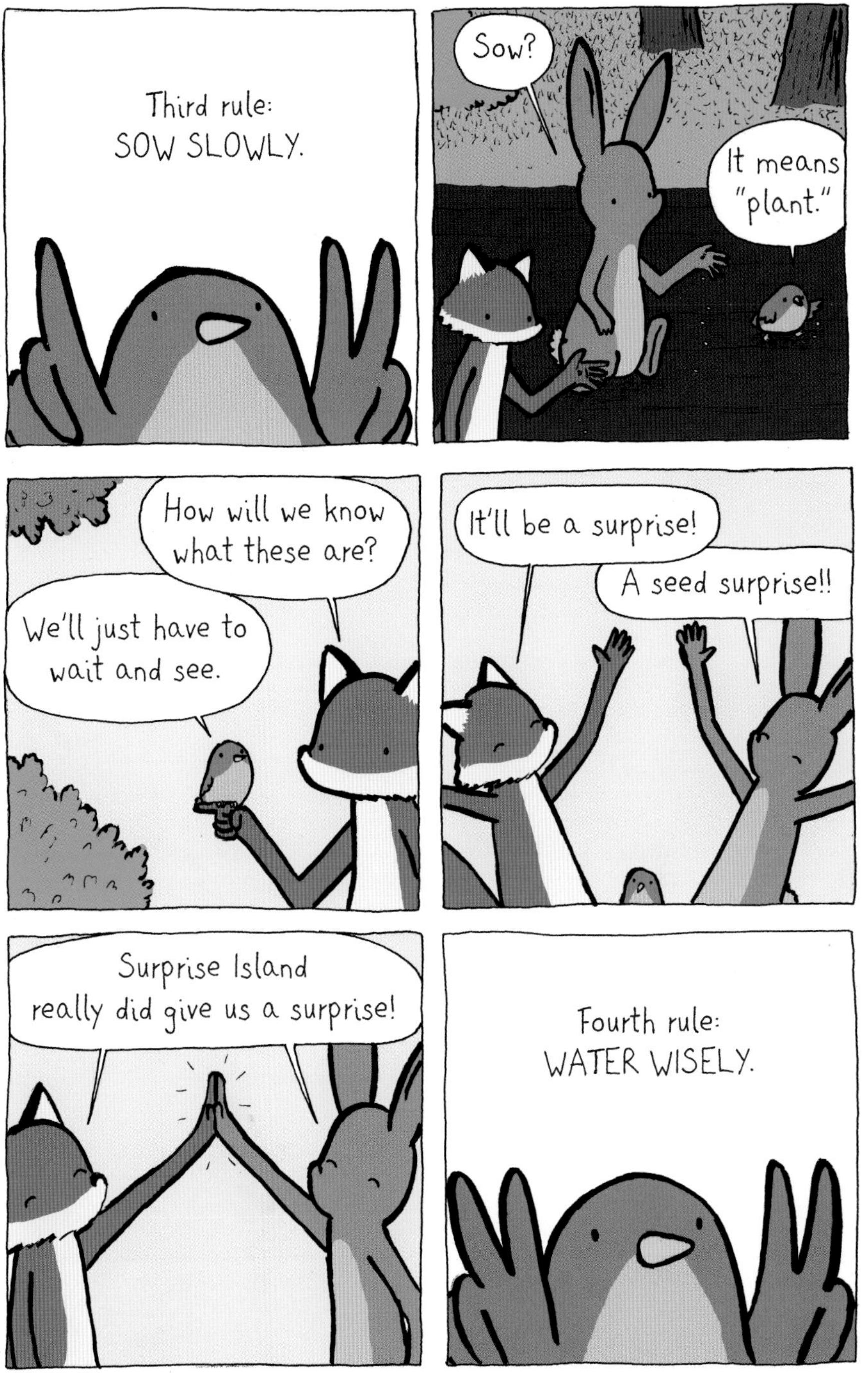
Third rule:
SOW SLOWLY.
Sow?
It means "plant."
How will we know what these are?
We'll just have to wait and see.
It'll be a surprise!
A seed surprise!!
Surprise Island really did give us a surprise!
Fourth rule:
WATER WISELY.

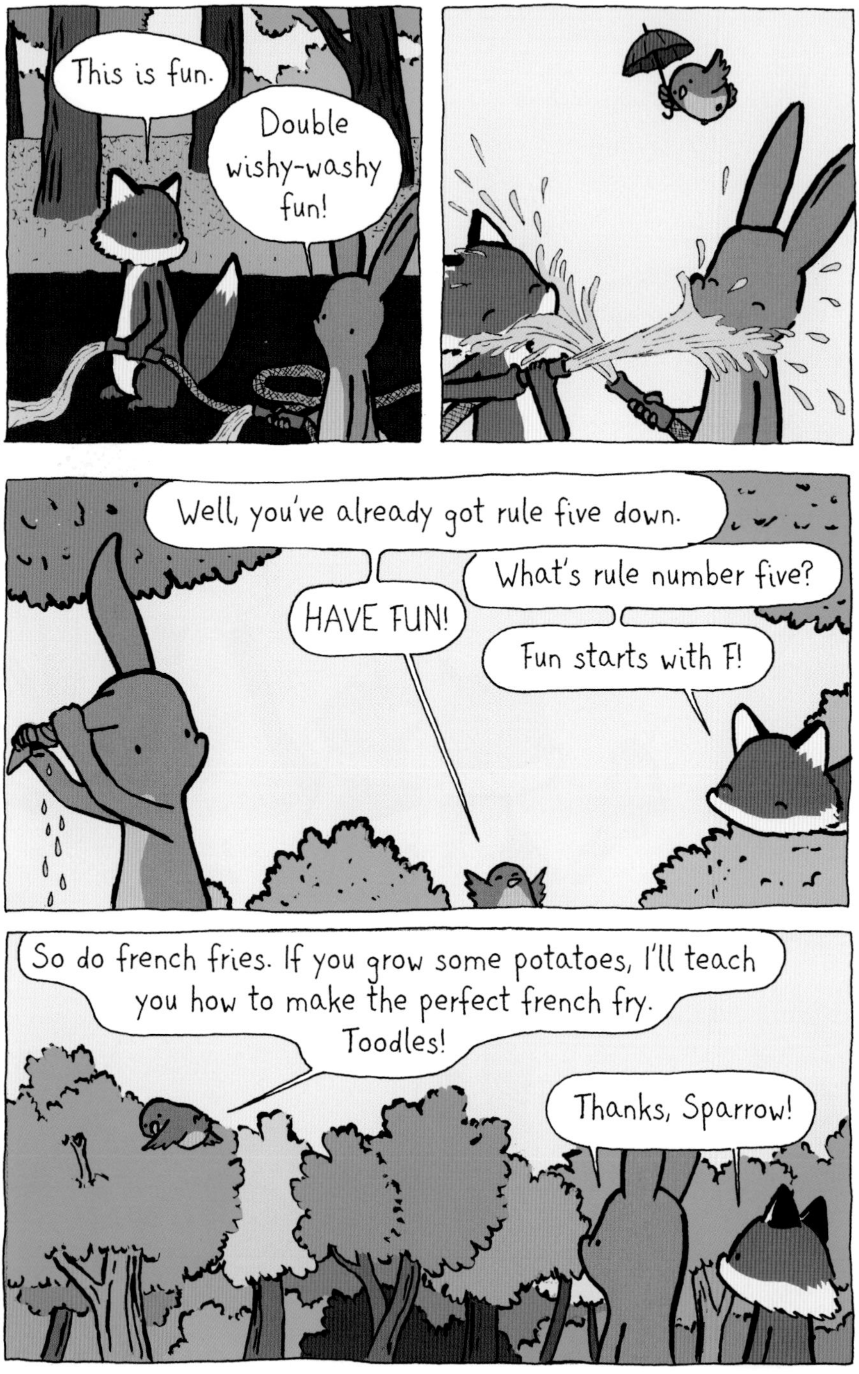
This is fun.
Double wishy-washy fun!
Well, you've already got rule five down.
What's rule number five?
HAVE FUN!
Fun starts with F!
So do french fries. If you grow some potatoes, I'll teach you how to make the perfect french fry. Toodles!
Thanks, Sparrow!

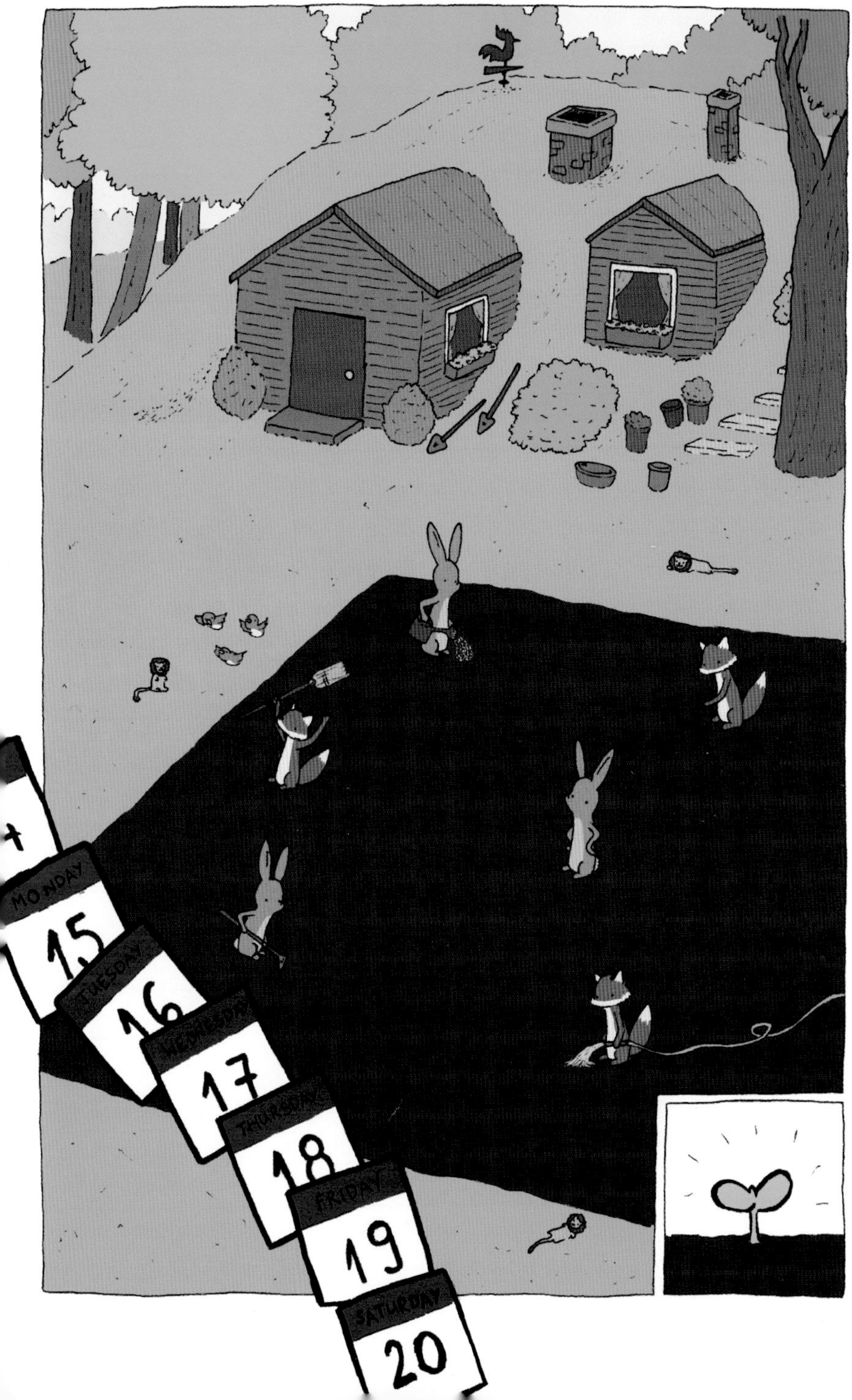
MONDAY
15
TUESDAY
16
WEDNESDAY
17
THURSDAY
18
FRIDAY
19
SATURDAY
20

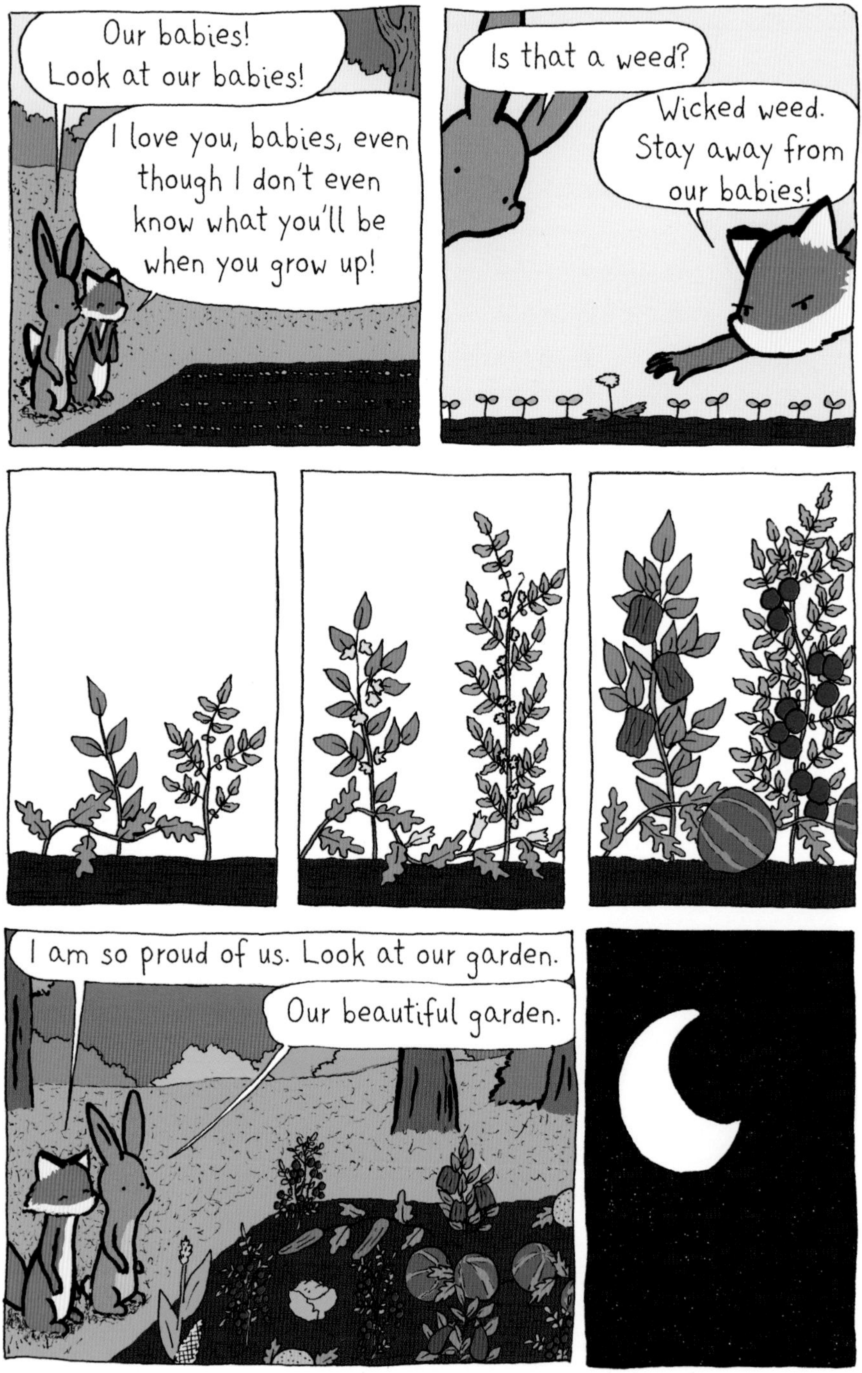
Our babies! Look at our babies!
I love you, babies, even though I don't even know what you'll be when you grow up!
Is that a weed?
Wicked weed. Stay away from our babies!
I am so proud of us. Look at our garden.
Our beautiful garden.

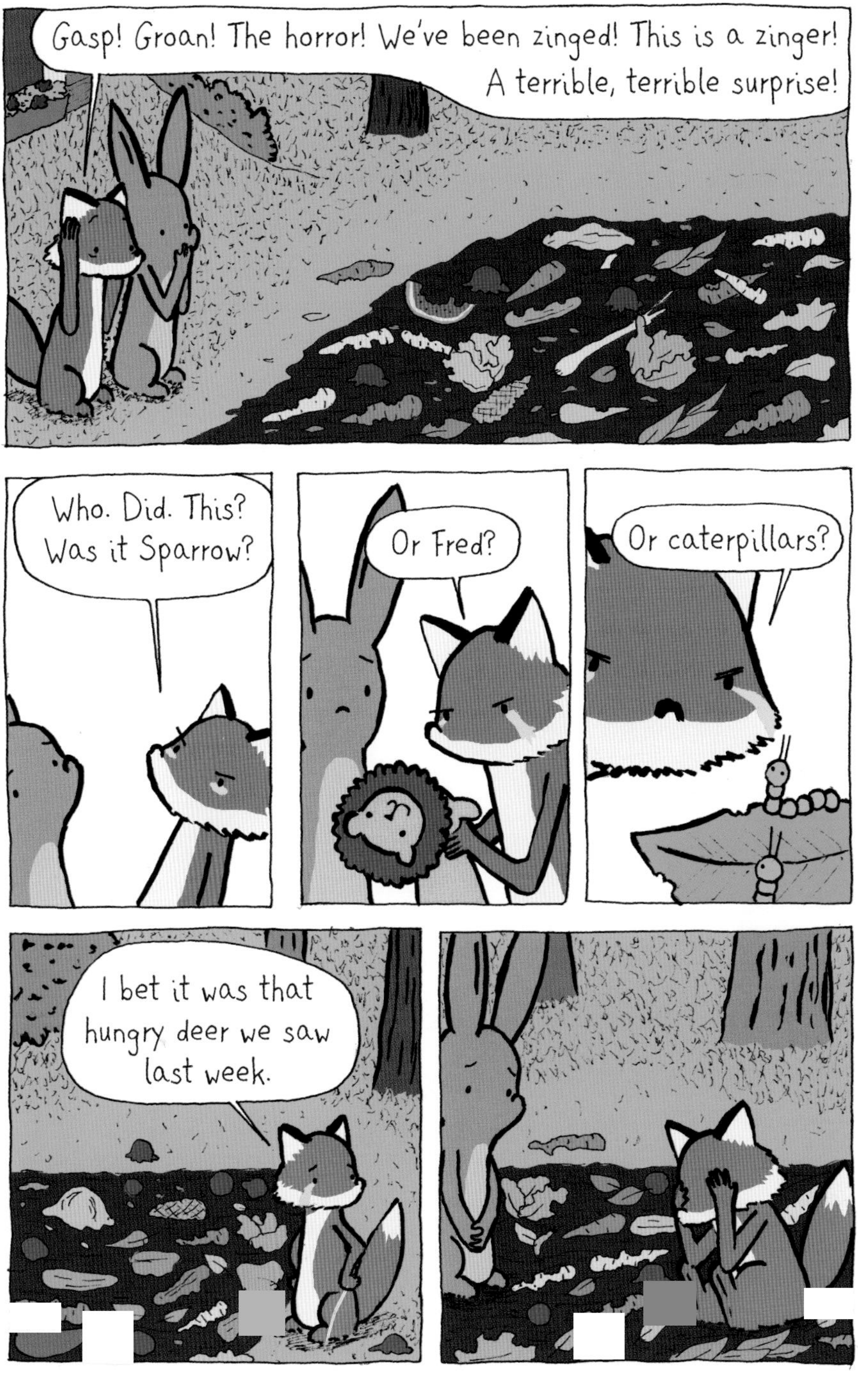
Gasp! Groan! The horror! We've been zinged! This is a zinger! A terrible, terrible surprise!
Who. Did. This? Was it Sparrow?
Or Fred?
Or caterpillars?
I bet it was that hungry deer we saw last week.

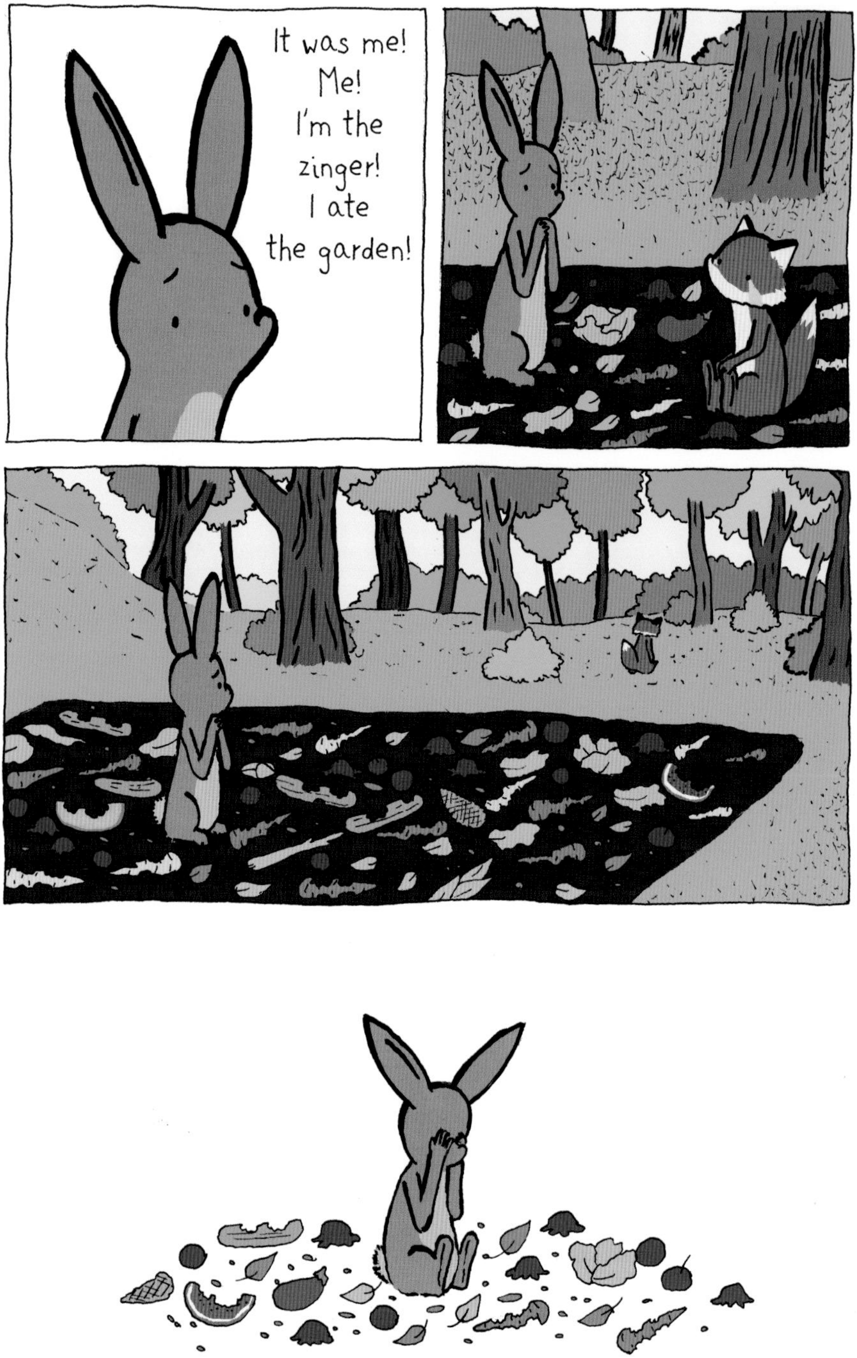
It was me! Me! I'm the zinger! I ate the garden!

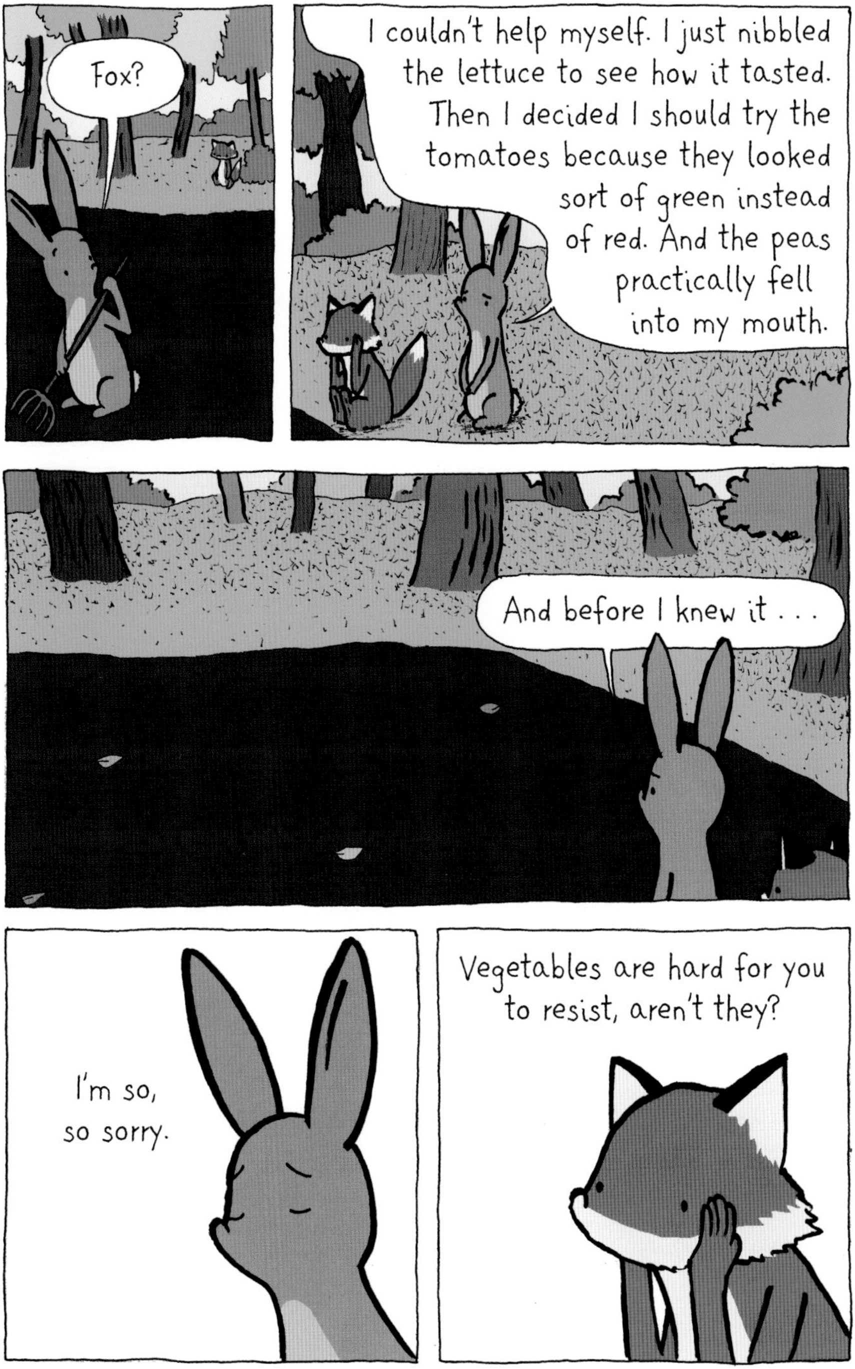
Fox?
I couldn't help myself. I just nibbled the lettuce to see how it tasted. Then I decided I should try the tomatoes because they looked sort of green instead of red. And the peas practically fell into my mouth.
And before I knew it . . .
I'm so, so sorry.
Vegetables are hard for you to resist, aren't they?

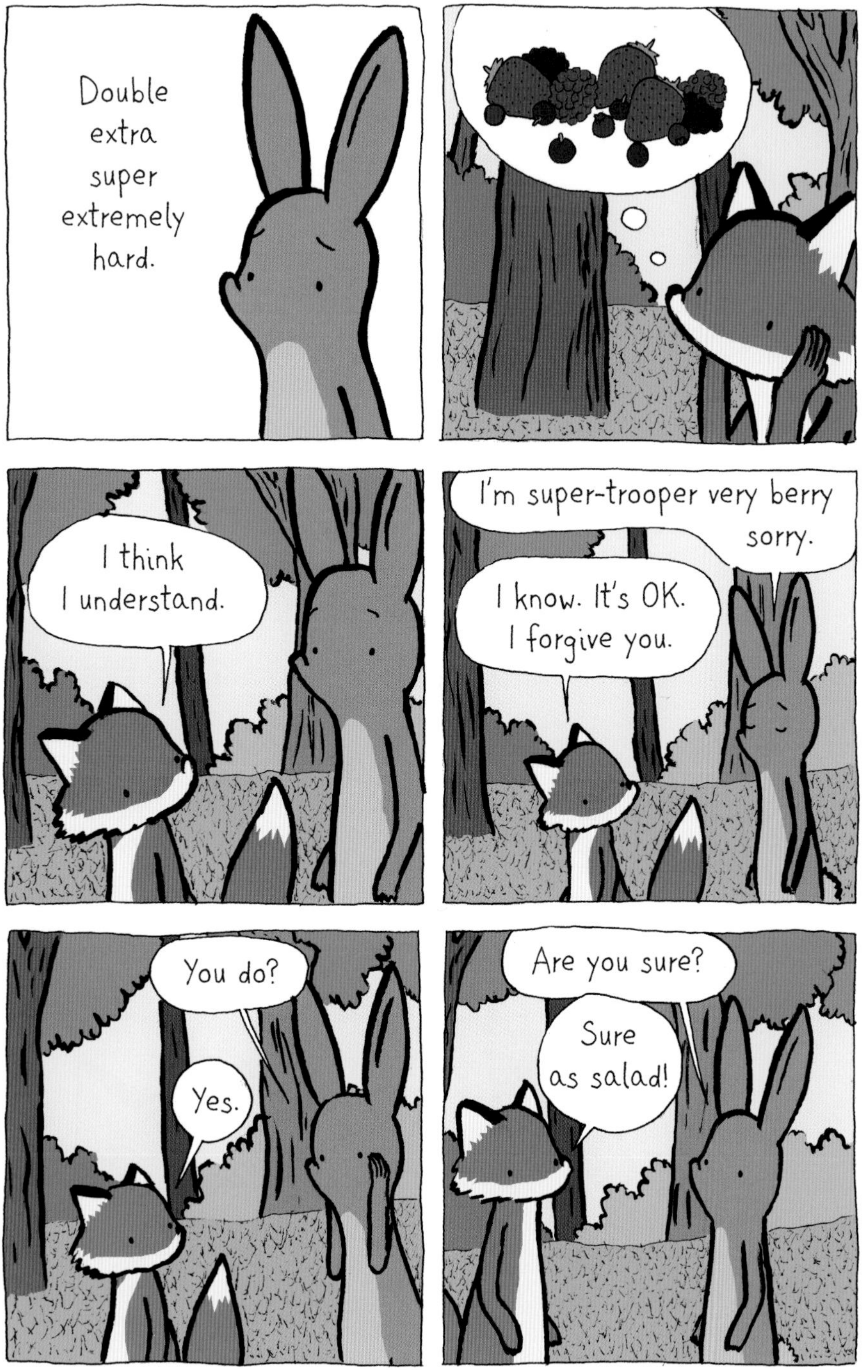
Double extra super extremely hard.
I think I understand.
I'm super-trooper very berry sorry.
I know. It's OK. I forgive you.
You do?
Yes.
Are you sure?
Sure as salad!

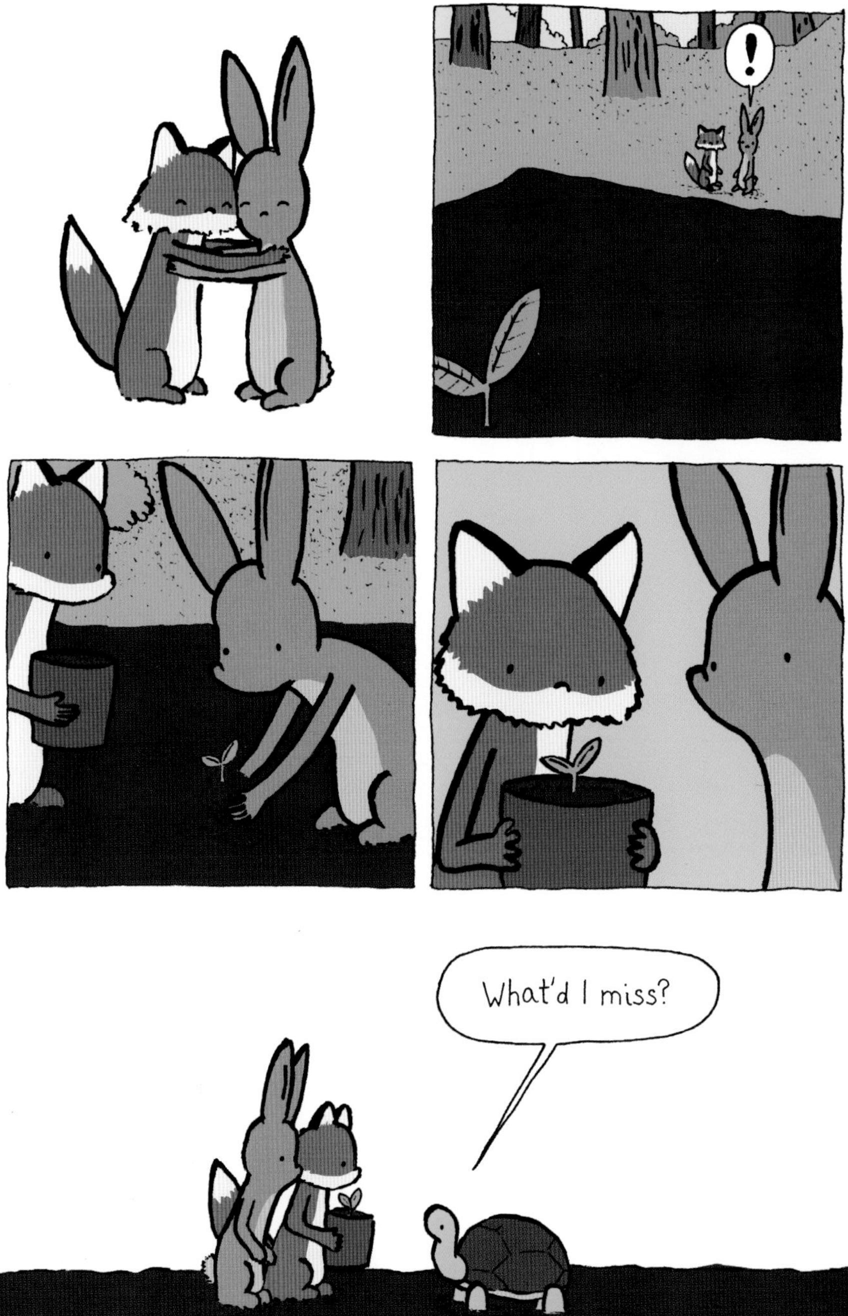
!
What'd I miss?

STORY FIVE

SQUEEZE, SWEET & SOUR

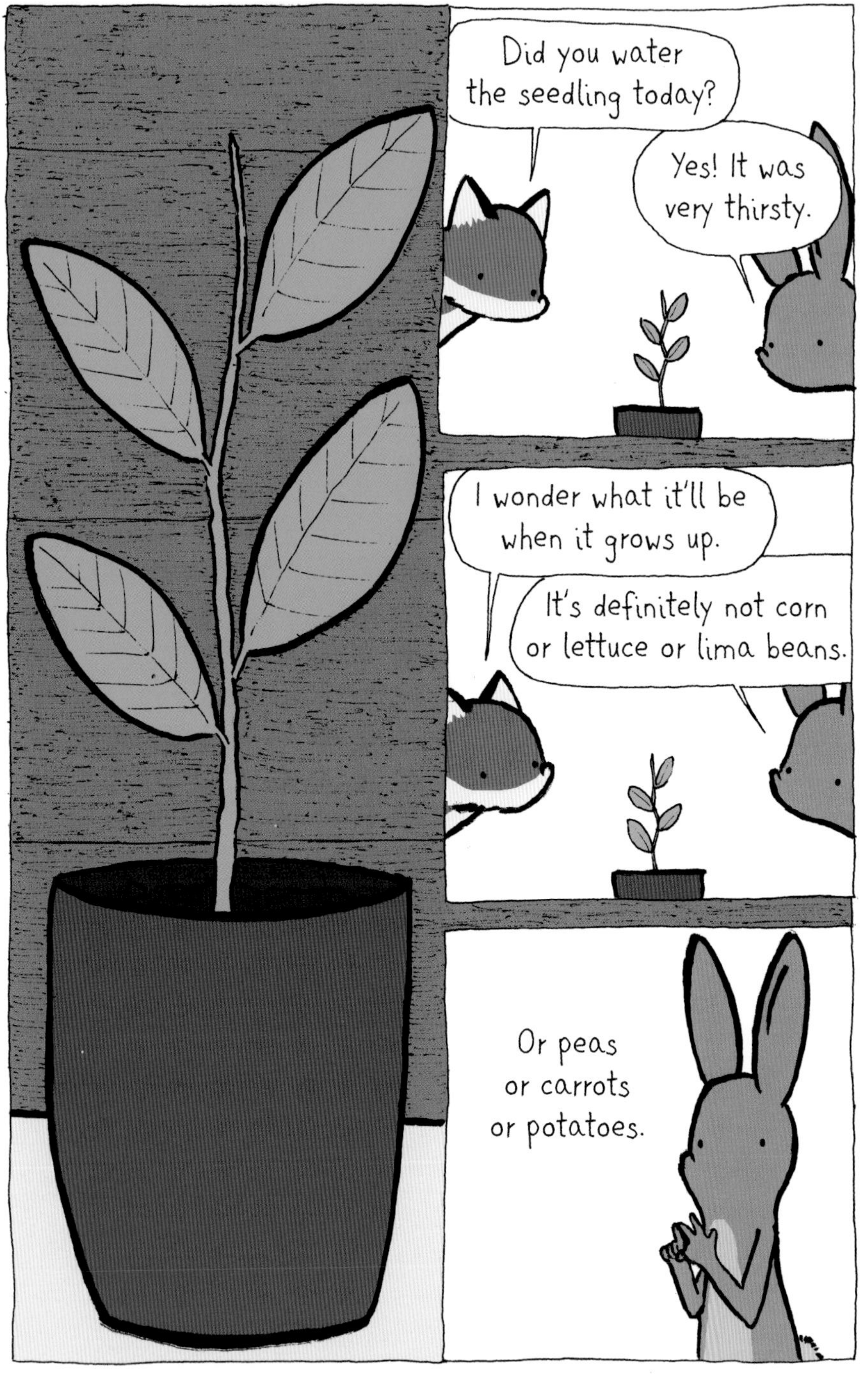
Did you water the seedling today?
Yes! It was very thirsty.
I wonder what it'll be when it grows up.
It's definitely not corn or lettuce or lima beans.
Or peas or carrots or potatoes.

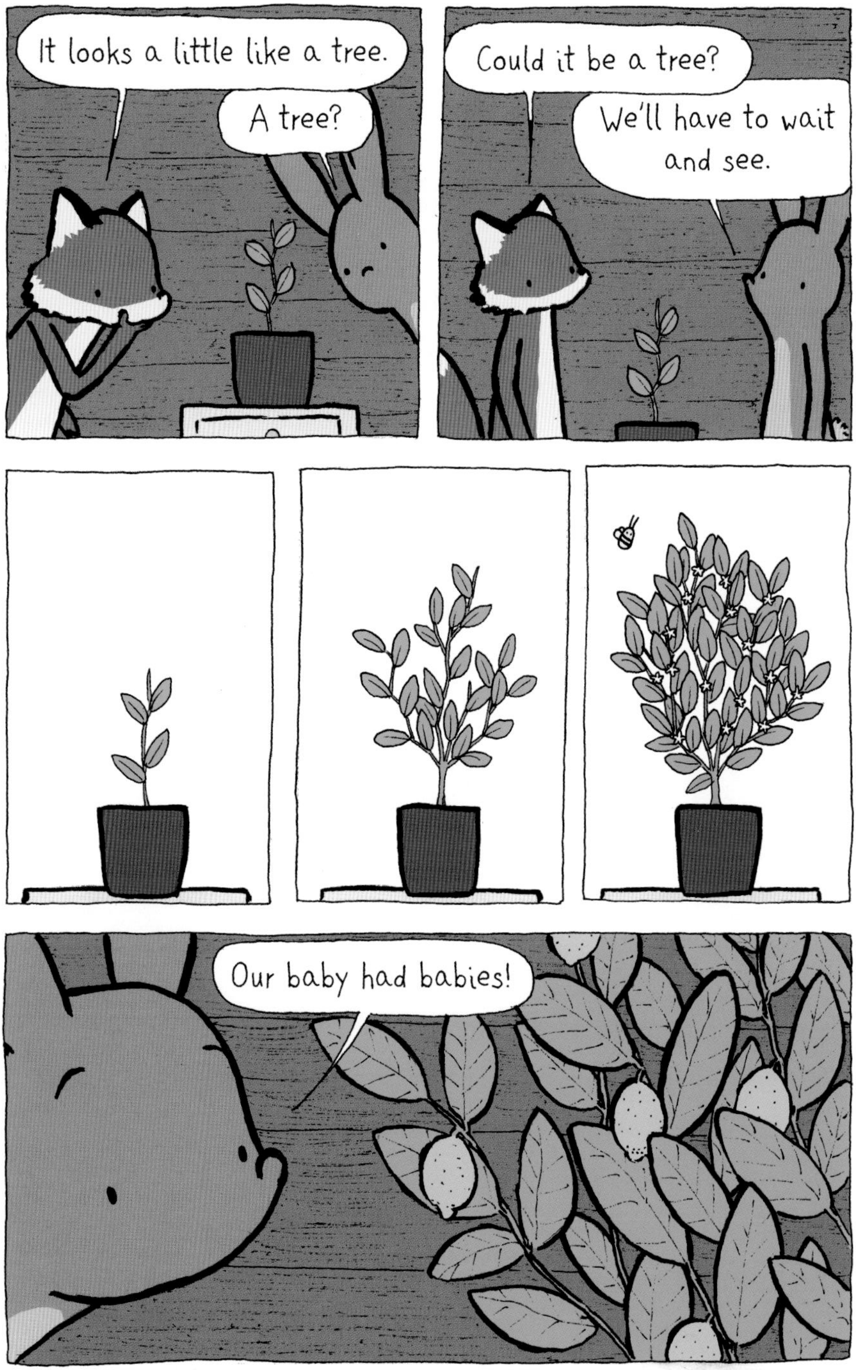
It looks a little like a tree.
A tree?
Could it be a tree?
We'll have to wait and see.
Our baby had babies!

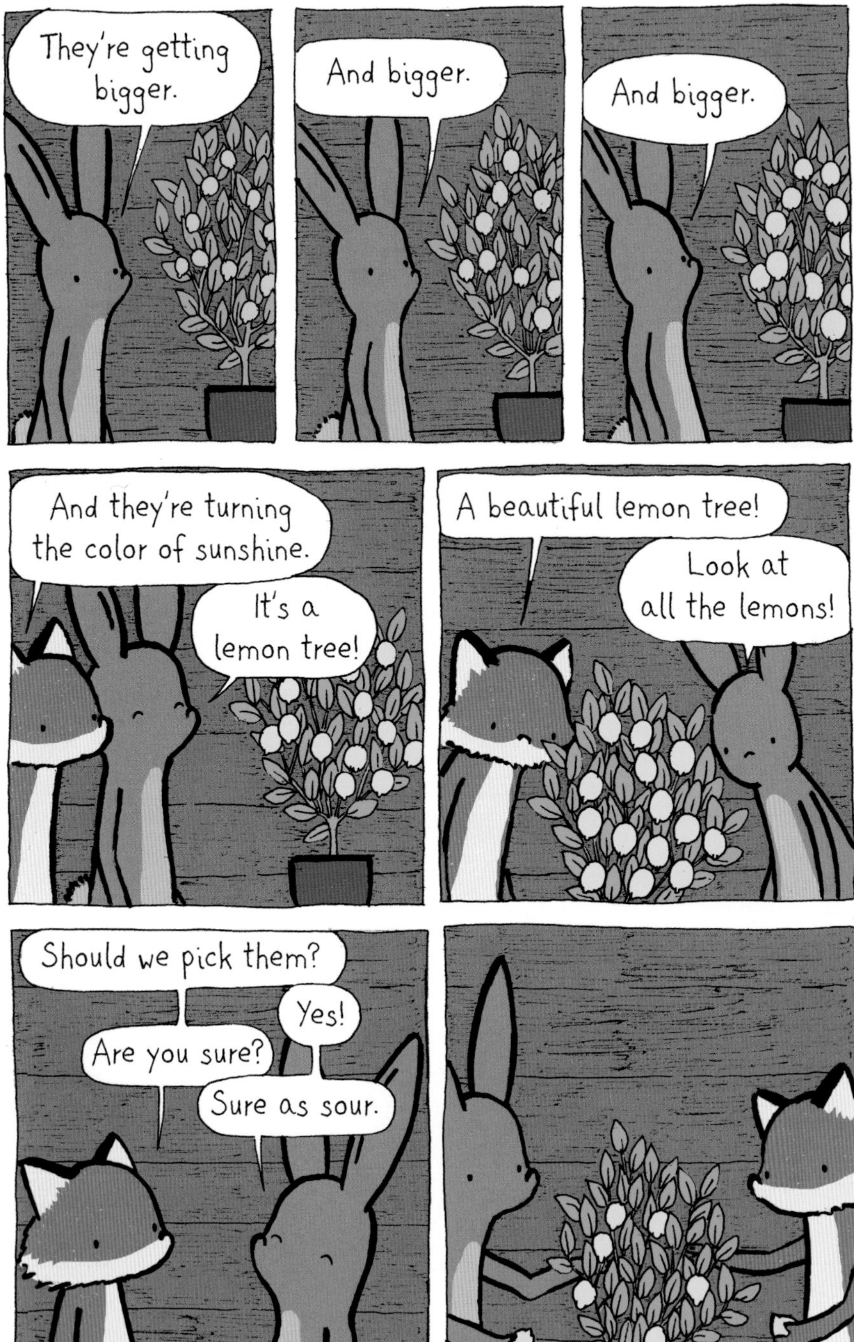
They're getting bigger.
And bigger.
And bigger.
And they're turning the color of sunshine.
It's a lemon tree!
A beautiful lemon tree!
Look at all the lemons!
Should we pick them?
Yes!
Are you sure?
Sure as sour.

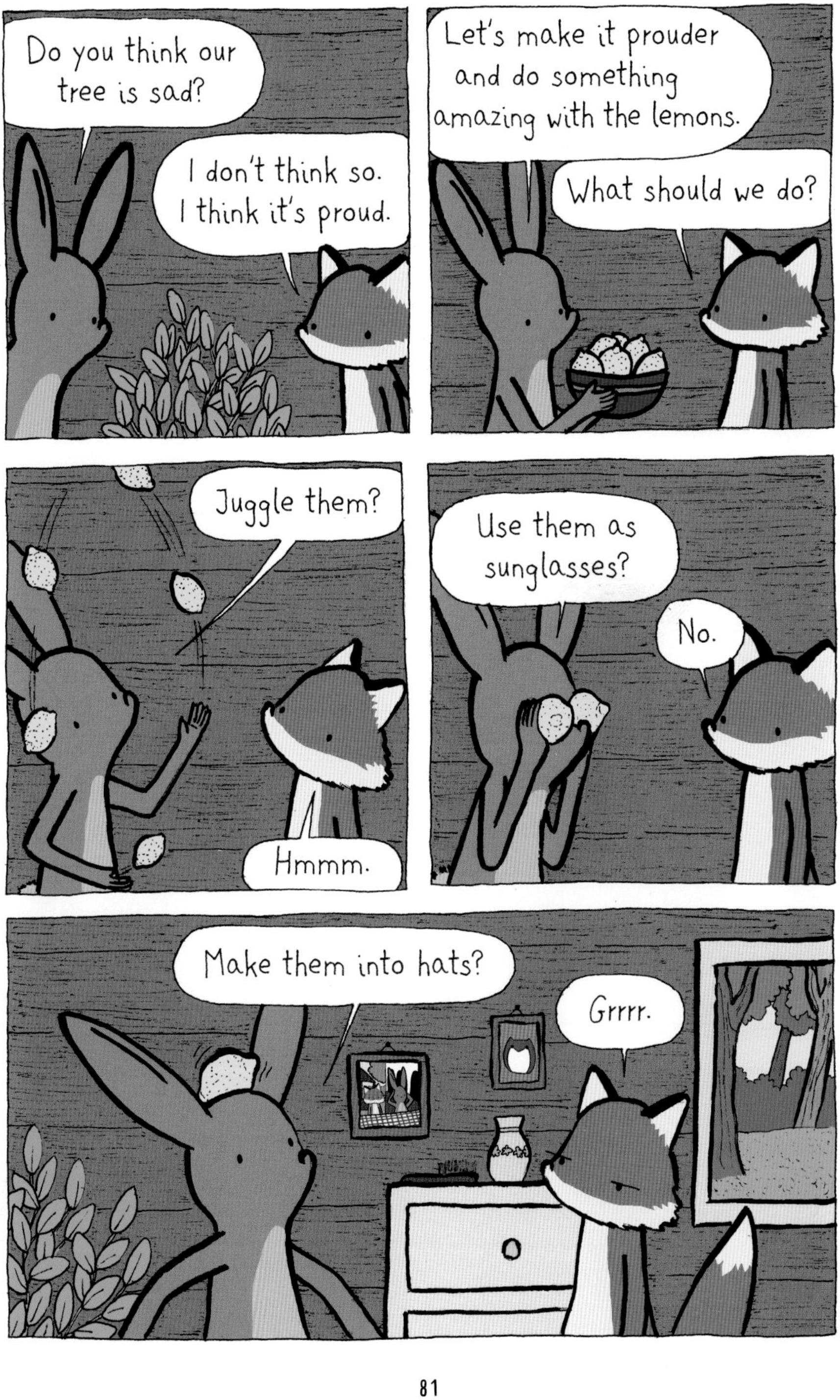
Do you think our tree is sad?
I don't think so. I think it's proud.
Let's make it prouder and do something amazing with the lemons.
What should we do?
Juggle them?
Hmmm.
Use them as sunglasses?
No.
Make them into hats?
Grrrr.

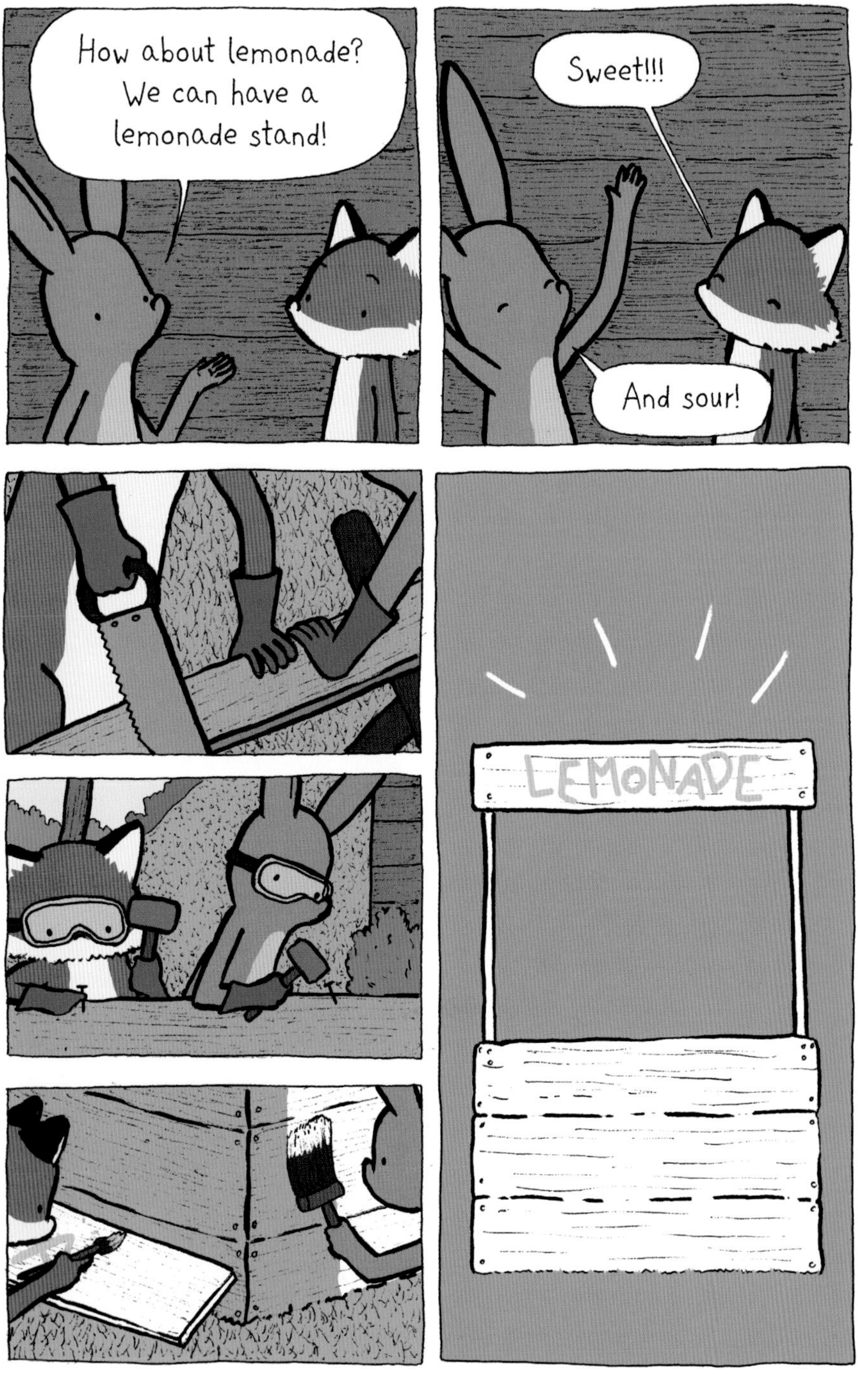
How about lemonade? We can have a lemonade stand!
Sweet!!!
And sour!
LEMONADE

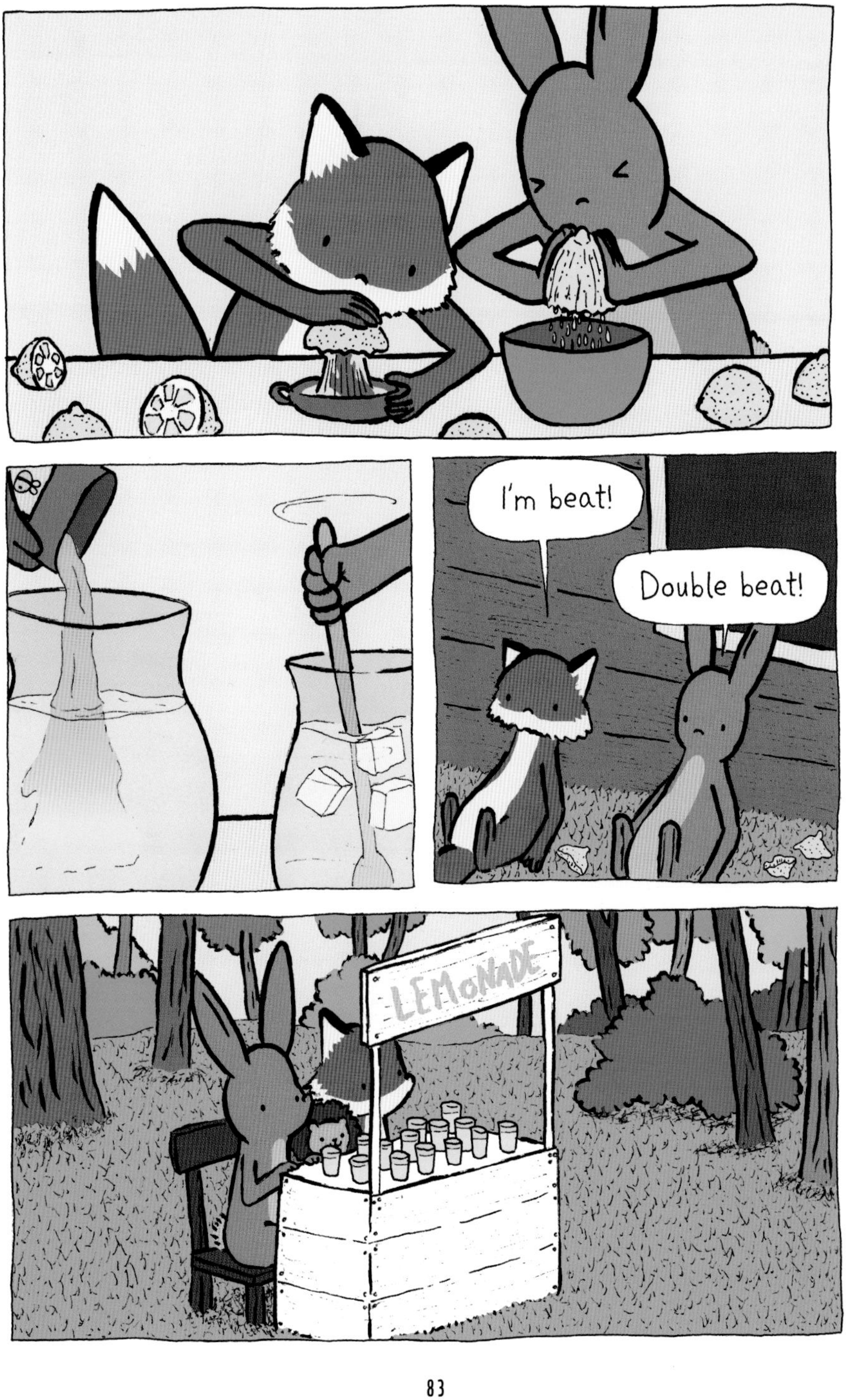
I'm beat!
Double beat!
LEMONADE

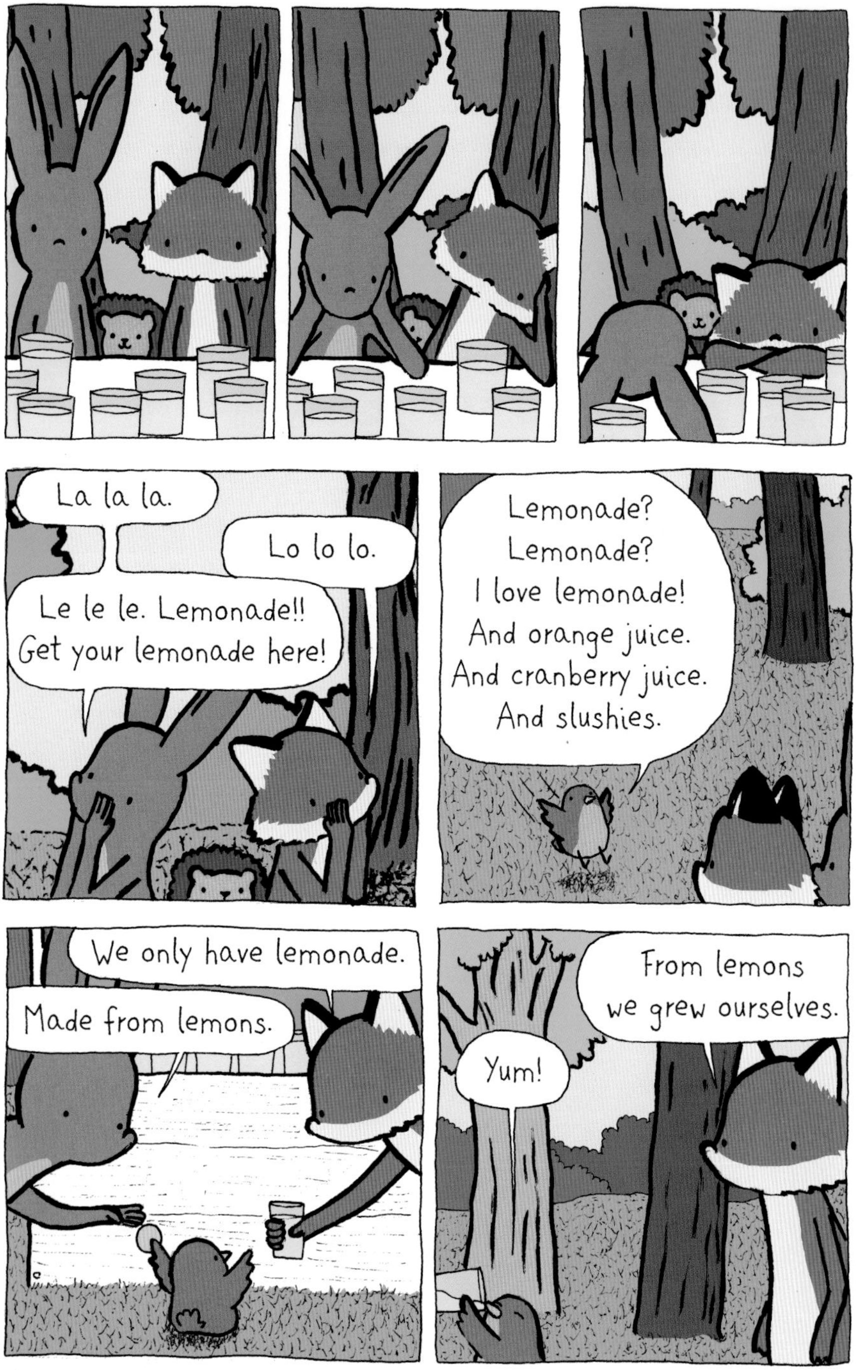
La la la.
Lo lo lo.
Le le le. Lemonade!! Get your lemonade here!
Lemonade? Lemonade? I love lemonade! And orange juice. And cranberry juice. And slushies.
We only have lemonade.
Made from lemons.
From lemons we grew ourselves.
Yum!

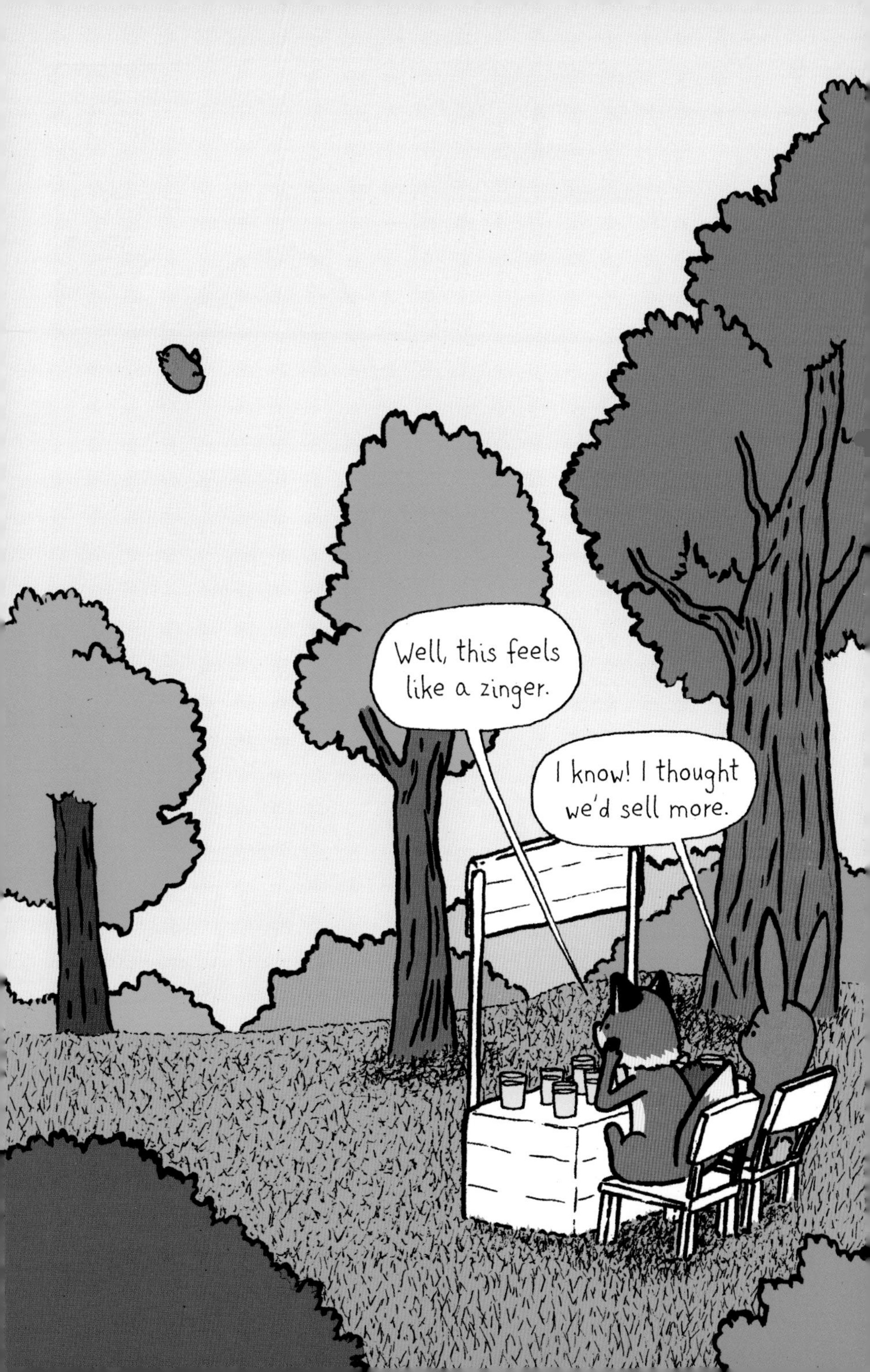
Well, this feels like a zinger.
I know! I thought we'd sell more.

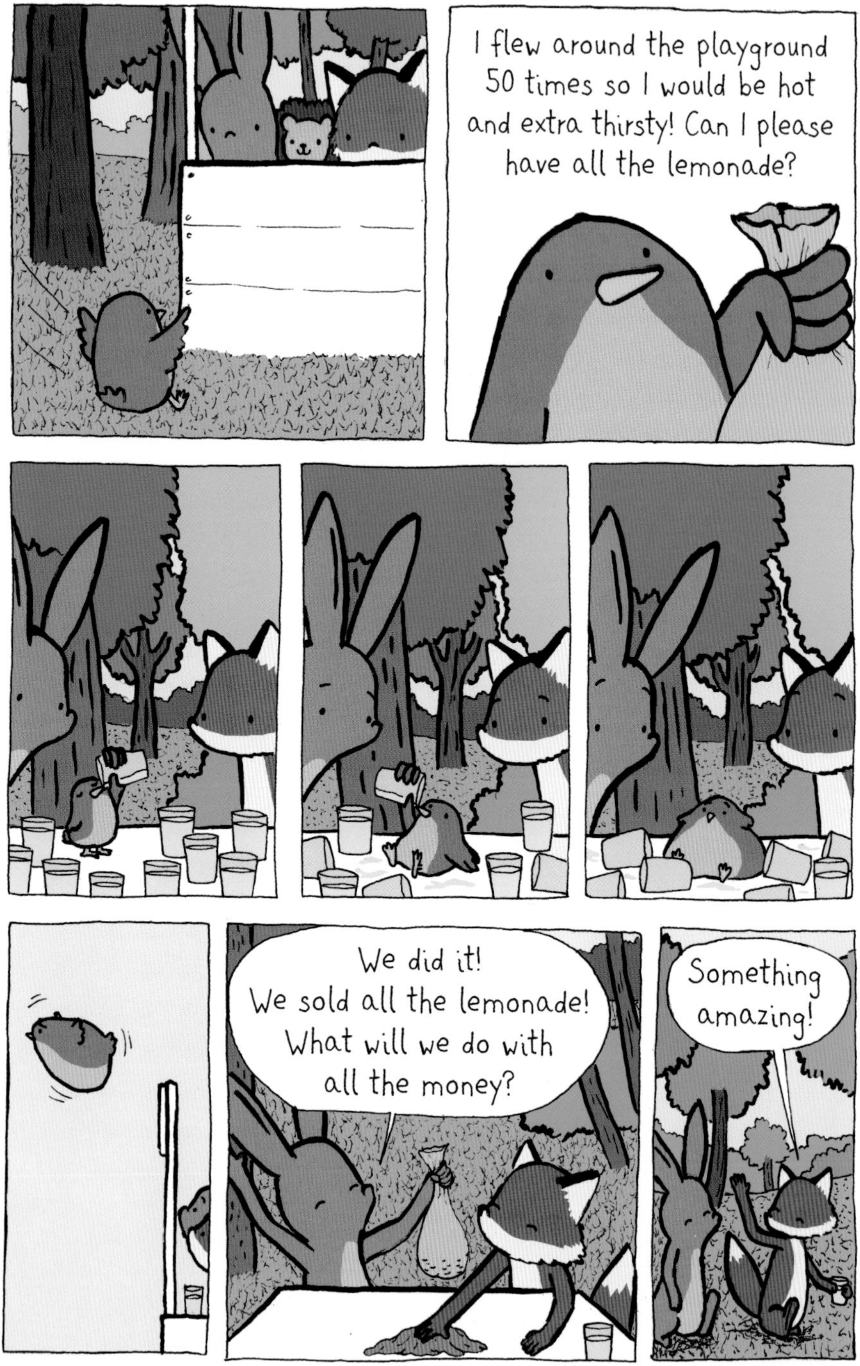
I flew around the playground 50 times so I would be hot and extra thirsty! Can I please have all the lemonade?
We did it! We sold all the lemonade! What will we do with all the money?
Something amazing!

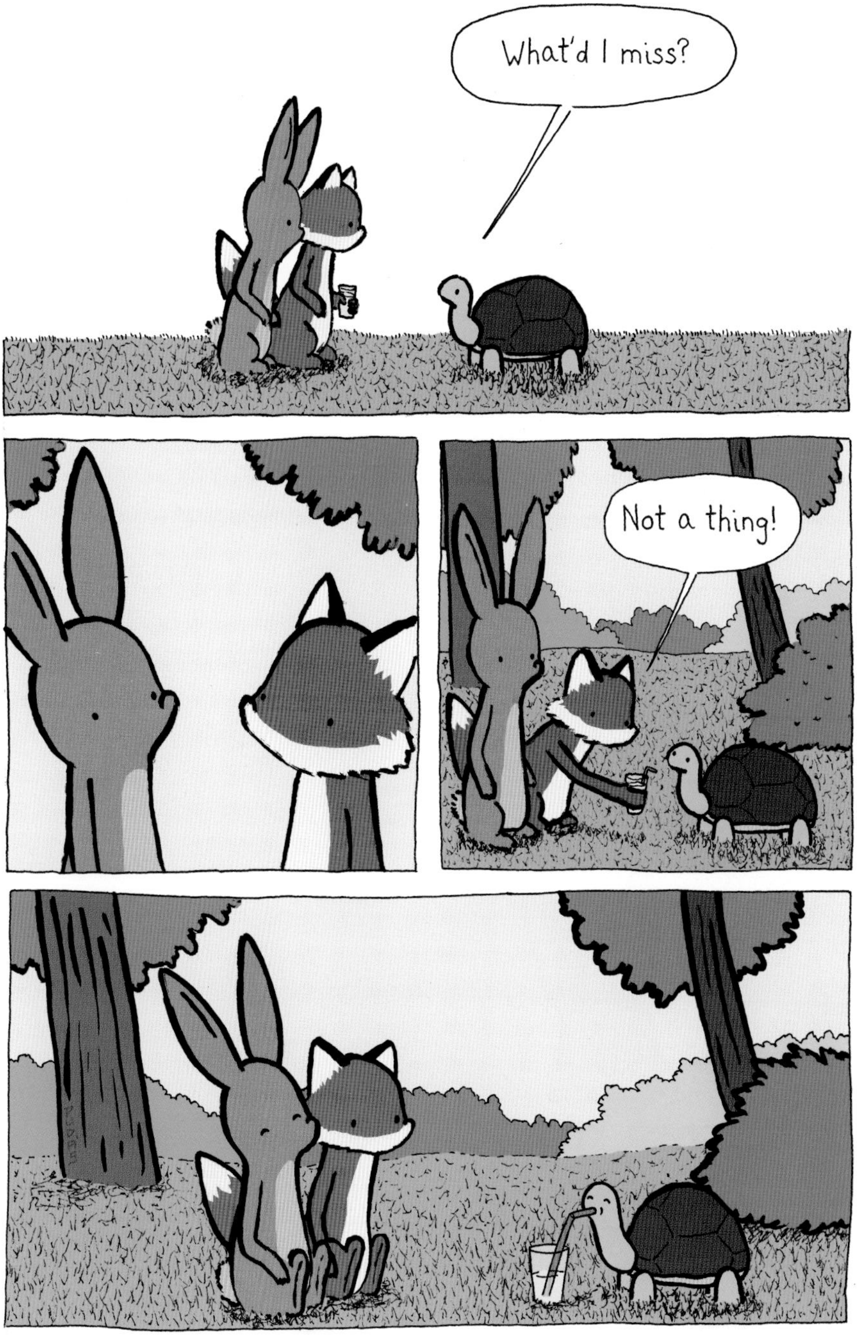
What'd I miss?
Not a thing!

ABOUT THE AUTHOR

Beth Ferry is as sure as sand and salt water and sunshine that living by the beach in New Jersey is the perfect place for her. The stories in this book were inspired by the adventures of her three children as they explored their little slice of the world. Sparrow would contend that the best slice in life is a pizza slice, and Beth would have to agree; she completely relates to Sparrow, who is a true adventurer when it comes to food. Beth is the author of many books for young readers, including *Caveboy Crush*, *The Scarecrow*, and the *New York Times* bestselling *Stick and Stone*. Like Fox, she believes in fun and family and friends, which all start with the awesome letter F. You can learn more at bethferry.com.

ABOUT THE ILLUSTRATOR

Gergely Dudás is a self-taught illustrator. The name Dudás means *bagpiper*, but he is not (yet) a self-taught bagpiper, though he does play a few other instruments. Gergely was born in July 1991. In his first few years of working, his art style was a lot more abstract than it is today. He is the creator of the Bear's Book of Hidden Things seek-and-find series.

Like Fox and Rabbit, Gergely loves adventures big and small. And, like Sparrow, he loves all kinds of food (except liver and eggplant). He lives with his girlfriend, a dog, and a dwarf rabbit called Fahéj, which means *cinnamon*. He has more pocket watches than pockets.

Gergely's work is inspired by the magic of the natural world. You can see more from him at dudolf.com.

FOR ANNIE, A WONDERFUL WRITER
AND A SUPER-TROOPER FRIEND
—B.F.

A BOOK ABOUT FRIENDSHIP
FOR MY DEAR FRIEND, BARNI
—G.D.

The art in this book was created with graphite and ink and colored digitally.

PUBLISHER'S NOTE: This is a work of fiction. Names, characters, places,
and incidents are either the product of the author's imagination or used
fictitiously, and any resemblance to actual persons, living or dead,
business establishments, events, or locales is entirely coincidental.

Cataloging-in-Publication Data has been applied for and may be
obtained from the Library of Congress.

ISBN 978-1-4197-4077-0

Text copyright © 2020 Beth Ferry
Illustrations copyright © 2020 Gergely Dudás
Book design by Steph Stilwell

Printed and bound in China
10 9 8 7 6 5 4 3 2 1

Amulet Books are available at special discounts when purchased in quantity for premiums and
promotions as well as fundraising or educational use. Special editions can also be created to
specification. For details, contact specialsales@abramsbooks.com or the address below.

Amulet Books® is a registered trademark of Harry N. Abrams, Inc.

ABRAMS The Art of Books
195 Broadway, New York, NY 10007
abramsbooks.com